SHRINK-WRAPPED MURDER

BY

JOHN P. PALMER

Other books available from Amazon by John P. Palmer:

- **2605**

  Fred Young is late for a meeting at the World Trade Centre and decides to let everyone think he was killed. He begins a new life as he tries to find himself. (2018)
- **Susan's Story**

  Fred's wife, Susan Young is devasted when her husband is apparently killed by the terrorist attacks. She and her children struggle to adjust to losing him, but she inherits a fortune. The way she handles herself and her fortune leads to her election as a Senator. (2020)
- **Murder at the Office Christmas Party**

  Linda Batchly is the no-nonsense CEO of Arttekko, a firm that mass produces art for hotel rooms and offices. The people working for her fear her, but they like their jobs. Finally, her pushy manner becomes too much, and she is murdered. (2020)
- **Three Murder Mysteries: *scripts for mystery dinner theatre plays***

  Scripts for evenings of fun, laughter, and mysteries, along with a chapter on how to produce, direct, and act in mystery dinner theatre plays (2019)

Shrink-Wrapped Murder

Chapter 1 – Making an Entrance

Crash!

Dr. James Melrose fell against the door and staggered into the hotel conference room. His forehead was bruised and cut, and he was bleeding from the corner of his mouth. He took a few steps into the room and crumpled onto the floor. Everyone in the large conference room gasped, momentarily frozen in place.

As people were leaving their seats to see what they could do to help him, his long-time assistant Phillipa MaGraw came through the door. She saw him lying on the floor and screamed. "Oh my God! What happened? Dr. Melrose, are you okay?"

She threw her shoulder bag onto a chair and knelt down to take his pulse.

"He doesn't have a pulse!" she exclaimed. "What happened?"

She looked around anxiously and continued shouting, "What happened to Dr. Melrose? What happened?"

Shari McBride, a counsellor from Des Moines, Iowa, had been sitting right next to where Dr. Melrose fell. She got up nervously and was standing next to where his body lay on the floor, looking down at him but not doing anything.

"He staggered in here," she spluttered, "and then he fell. Is he going to be okay?"

"No!" Phillipa yelled, glaring at Shari, "I just told you, *he doesn't have a pulse.* He's dead! Can't you see that?"

Phillipa continued yelling at the people sitting around where Dr. Melrose had fallen. "How did he get this bruise and this cut on his forehead? Why is there some blood coming from the corner of his mouth? What happened? Tell me! What happened?"

Just then, Dr. Robin Bobbitt, noted television counselor and therapist on the program 'Round Pegs, Round Holes', entered the conference room from the hallway, where he had gone to take a phone call. He looked down at Dr. Melrose and exclaimed, "Oh, for Pete's sake, James! Get up! Or are you drunk, **again**!? Good grief..."

Phillipa interrupted him, "NO! He's *not* drunk! He collapsed and he doesn't have a pulse! Give him mouth-to-mouth or CPR or do something, Robin!"

Robin quickly glanced around the room and then knelt to check Dr. Melrose's pulse again.

Phillipa was livid. "I already *told* you he doesn't have a pulse! You don't have to check it, too. I know what I'm doing!"

Robin stood up and was about to reply when Dr. Andrew Kopfmann returned from the restroom, where he had gone to look for Dr. Melrose. Looking at the others but not noticing Dr. Melrose on the floor, he asked, "Have any of you seen Dr. Melrose? He wasn't in the men's room when I went to look for him there, but there was some blood on the front edge of the wash basin..."

Then he looked down at the floor and saw what everyone else was staring at. "Oh no!! what's wrong? What happened?"

Phillipa pointed to Shari, "According to this woman, he just staggered in here and collapsed! I think he's dead! He doesn't have a pulse!"

She rushed over to Andy and grabbed his arm, "What are we going to do, Andy? I need you to help me! Please!!!"

Andy patted her hand, trying to calm her, and then turned to the others in the convention room, "Is there a doctor in the house?"

He was embarrassed to ask such a clichéd question, but still, it made sense to him to ask it anyway.

Without thinking, Phillipa said, "Andy, you're all doctors, aren't you?"

She was mostly right. The proposed speakers for that session's panel discussion all had PhDs, as did many

5

of the members of the audience, but their PhDs were in psychology and related fields; they weren't MDs.

"Not a PhD-type doctor! I mean 'Is there a **real** doctor in the house?'"

Dr. Benjamin Bassett stepped forward. "I'm a physician," he said. "Let me examine him."

Dr. Bassett was a short, rotund man in a blue pinstripe three-piece suit. He strained to bend down to look at the body and finally just collapsed onto one knee, and as he did, his comb-over fell off to the right side of his head. After fussing with the body for a minute or two, Dr. Bassett struggled to stand up and was breathing heavily from the effort.

He brushed his hair back up over his head and announced, "He has a contusion on his forehead, and he has some blood dripping from the corner of his mouth. There appears to be some slight chafing around his neck. Also, his heart isn't beating. He's dead, but I can't tell whether his death was caused by that blow to his head or by something else."

Phillipa couldn't control herself.

"Why thank you **ever** so much for your expert opinion, doctor," she said, dripping with sarcasm. "It has been **so** helpful!"

Just then Dr. Ruth Westover sauntered into the room.

Seeing that people weren't all sitting in their chairs looking at the head table or gathered around the bar, she sensed a 'situation' and asked, "What's going on?

I ducked through the kitchen to get away from Andy and Robin, and then I stepped out into the back alley for a quick toke with someone from the kitchen staff." She glared across the room at Andy Kopfmann and Robin Bobbit in turn.

"Look here, Ruthie," Phillipa answered, gesturing toward the body that was barely visible through the legs of everyone hovering around it. "It looks as if Dr. Melrose was hit on the head or something. He collapsed right here, and now he's not breathing!"

Ruthie was annoyed. She was annoyed at Andy for having followed her around everywhere, annoyed at Robin for trying to chat her up all evening, annoyed at Phillipa for seeming to be in charge, and annoyed with Dr. Melrose for a whole host of things. She had been planning some academic fireworks with her presentation later that evening, during which she would bluntly and seriously contradict some long-standing research done by Dr. Melrose nearly forty years ago. She realized immediately that the session wouldn't be going ahead as planned, and she was peeved, to put it mildly.

- - -

Meanwhile Dr. Rich Murphy was the first member of the audience to call 9-1-1.

"I think Dr. James Melrose was hit on the head and killed," he drawled. "We're at the Midwest meeting of the Association of Sexual Psychologists, and we were about to have a panel presentation when Dr. Melrose staggered into the room and collapsed."

"Where are you?"

"Oh, I'm sorry, Ma'am. We're at the Jericho Hilton, here in downtown Jericho, Illinois. This is the conference hotel for our association. Dr. Melrose is lying on the floor here in the Lincoln Room up on the second floor. It's one of the rooms we're using for presentations at the conference."

"Don't let anyone leave the room," the 9-1-1 operator told him, "and don't let anyone touch anything or the victim. Got that?"

"Yes, Ma'am."

Rich turned to the fifty or so people in the room and shouted, "The police at 9-1-1 say no one is to leave, and no one is to touch anything. Okay, y'all?"

He returned to the phone. "Anything else, Ma'am?"

"May I have your name, sir?"

"Oh, sure. I'm sorry, Ma'am. I'm Dr. Richard Thomas Murphy, and I'm from Hot Springs University in Arkansas..."

"You say he was killed by a blow to the head. Be sure to explain that carefully to the investigators when they arrive."

"Yes, Ma'am, and thank you."

8

Chapter 2 – Containment

Rich Murphy kept an eye on the door to the room, but he had no intention of trying to stop anyone from leaving. As he later told the investigating officers, "... sure as shootin' I wasn't gonna try to stop anyone, but I was gonna take a photo on my cellphone of anyone who decided to leave."

Five minutes later, Patrolmen Donald Keene and Gerald Miller showed up. On the force, they were known as the Bobbsey Twins. They had gone through cadet training together, they were both 6'1", they both weighed about 205 pounds, and they both had hair the color of wet sand. The most noticeable differences were that Keene had green eyes and Miller's were brown, and they led separate lives when they were off duty, living at opposite ends of the city. On duty, though, they were known to be in sync with each other.

As they entered the room, they weren't sure what to expect, other than a dead body somewhere. Most of the people in the room were quietly milling about. Some had gathered around the body and were staring down at it, some were at the bar refreshing their drinks, and others were sitting together in small clusters. Everyone was talking in hushed tones and glancing at the body lying less than fifteen feet inside the door.

Patrolman Miller quickly announced that no one was to touch anything, and no one was to leave the room.

Rich not-so-quietly drawled, "Yes, Sir. I told 'em all that. I made sure nobody left, but I can't guarantee nobody touched anything'."

Meanwhile, Patrolman Keene checked Dr. Melrose's pulse and confirmed that he was dead. He phoned Lieutenant Michael 'Mike' Randall, of homicide, who was already on his way to the scene.

"Lieutenant, it looks like it might be a suspicious death, and get this: there must be nearly fifty psychologists here. This is going to be **really** fun," he groaned.

Lieutenant Randall arrived only five minutes later, along with Sergeants Jason Scheffler and Ellie Houston.

Sergeant Houston took in the scene. "Oh, this is just too wonderful – a large roomful of suspects. Well, let's make sure no one leaves before we can question them, and maybe we should even get ready to search them."

"Don't get ahead of things," cautioned Lieutenant Randall. "Let's wait until we hear what the medical examiner and forensics can tell us before we get into conducting body searches."

The Sergeants put crime scene tape around the area where the body was lying on the floor, using chairs to hold the tape, and while they were doing that, Lieutenant Randall addressed the room.

"Ladies and Gentlemen, I have to ask you to take no more photos, please, and put your smartphones away... or at the very least please don't post about this on social media until we have a better idea about what has happened."

"Imagine how you would feel if you learned about the death of a close friend or relative through some postings on Facebook or Twitter," he continued. "So please do not post anything about this yet.

"Sergeant Houston, call headquarters and get some more investigators sent over to help with the questioning. Ask for Newhouse and Steglitz, for sure, plus anyone else they can spare. And get the Butts and Holly teams up here, too."

Butts was Dr. Julie Butts, the Medical Examiner, and Holly was Bob Holly, head of forensics.

He turned back to address the room. "Now, who's in charge here?"

Phillipa approached the Lieutenant with some apparent hesitation and said, "Well ... this was going to be a session that I organized for Dr. Melrose, but he's dead ...."

She gestured to the body on the floor.

"And since I am ... or was ... his personal assistant, and since I did organize the session, I guess that leaves me in charge, in a way."

She quickly added, "But most of the others here have lots more authority and power than I do. I'm just an assistant; I'm not a licensed psychologist."

"Tell me what's going on," said Lieutenant Randall. "What was supposed to happen here?"

"Well, as you probably know, the Jericho Hilton is the conference center for this year's Midwest ASP meeting ..."

She saw the puzzled look on the lieutenant's face and explained, "Oh, ASP – that's the Association of Sexual Psychologists. It's been in the papers the past couple of days. There are as many as four different sessions going on at any one time in the different banquet or conference rooms here at the hotel. This was going to be just one of the sessions. Dr. Melrose wanted this session to be the last one in the evening, like this, after dinner, so we could have a wine-and-beer bar now and then serve hors d'oeuvres at the conclusion of the session."

"Do you know how he got the bruise and cut on his forehead?"

"No, I don't, but Andy – that's Dr. Kopfmann over there in the tweed sportcoat and pale pink shirt," Phillipa gestured toward Andy Kopfmann, "had gone to check on Dr. Melrose, and when he came back, he said there was blood on the wash basin in the men's room..."

"Thank you," said Lieutenant Randall. "Would you mind having a seat right here for a minute or two? Thanks."

Once again, Lieutenant Randall addressed the room, "Ladies and Gentlemen, please make yourselves as comfortable as possible. This sudden and

13

unexplained death of Dr. Melrose means we will have to talk with each of you at least once before you go home or back to your hotel rooms or wherever you'd like to go."

His announcement was met with groans, complaints, and murmurs. Most of the people there understood the situation once it was explained to them, but that didn't make them any happier. Several of them pulled out their cellphones to let spouses or friends know they'd be detained for a while, and, no, they had no idea how long it would be.

"While we're waiting, Keene and Miller, you've just earned temporary promotions; you're investigators for now and for the next day or two while we sort this out. Keene, you go find out which men's room has blood on the front of the wash basin. If you have to, get Dr. Kopfmann over there in the tweed and pink to go with you and point it out to you, but make sure you send him back to this room when you're done with him. Watch him and make sure he comes back here. Then seal off that men's room and wait there for forensics to join you; don't let anyone else in there, and don't let anyone who is in there use the washbasins.

"Miller, Sergeants Houston and Scheffler are going to need some help interviewing all these people, so you stay here and help them out. You know the drill. Start by asking people the basic questions – where they live, where they can be reached, phone numbers, email addresses, *et cetera*. And then ask what they saw, what they heard, and even what they suspect. You've tagged along on enough investigations that you're ready to do some on your own. Just be sure you keep good, legible notes. Take your time if you

14

have to, and make sure you put everything in your notes; there's no rush. Meanwhile, I'll find out a bit more from Ms. MaGraw."

- - -

For their initial interview, Lieutenant Randall led Phillipa over to a pair of chairs at the doorway, where he could more easily make sure no one left the room. He wanted to be there, too, to greet Dr. Butts and Bob Holly when they arrived.

He began by asking her, "Are all the sessions this posh? A wine and beer bar? Post-session hors d'oeuvres?"

"No, they aren't, and this one isn't all that posh either. I mean, it's a cash bar after all ... but the hors d'oeuvres were going to be nicer than just chips and dip for sure. This was going to be Dr. Melrose's farewell party in a way. He wasn't really retiring, but he was giving up his role in ASP – the Association, that is – as a session organizer, and he wanted to go out in style. That's why he lobbied so strongly to have this year's conference held here in Jericho, where he works... worked... and taught. He's – was – ..."

She paused a moment. "This is hard. I'm sorry. He *was* a psychologist here in town, and he *was* a professor of psychology here at Jericho State.

"Anyway, back to your question about this session. He liked portraying himself as a godfather, of sorts. He had carefully selected the panelists for this evening to make himself look good professionally; at least that's what he expected to happen, but it was pretty clear to most people here that the other

15

panelists didn't always support or agree with everything about Dr. Melrose's research."

"How were things proceeding? Had the presentations begun yet?"

"No, they hadn't. For some insane reason, the idiot hotel I-T staff confused the equipment requisitions and repair orders, and so we didn't have a projector ready here for Dr. Melrose's PowerPoint display. I think Andy Kopfmann was scheduled to do a PowerPoint slide show as well, and maybe the other panelists were, too – I'm not sure. Anyway, to fill the time while we were waiting for the equipment to arrive and get set up, Dr. Melrose did some formal introductions of the panelists and then encouraged everyone to mingle and have something to drink while we were waiting."

"Who are the other panelists?"

"Well, there's Andy ... that's Dr. Andrew Kopfmann."

"Where's he from and what's his specialty?"

"He's based in Vancouver, British Columbia, but he's doing a year-long project over in Liechtenstein --- that's in central Europe. Dr. Melrose wanted him to be here because his work on group dynamics seems to dovetail nicely with the work that Dr. Melrose did himself on sexuality and group dynamics many years ago."

Lieutenant Randall shifted gears. "How long have you been with Dr. Melrose?"

"Oh, ever since I graduated with an honors degree in psychology nearly twenty years ago. He was one of my professors, and he liked what I did in his classes so much that he offered me a temporary job that summer, right out of college; it grew into this."

"And just what does 'this' involve?" asked Lieutenant Randall. He wondered how much more was involved with 'this'. Had they ever been lovers? Had the glamor worn off for Phillipa during the past twenty years? How strong might her motive be for murdering him?

"Well, I keep track of his appointments; I compile his notes from his therapy sessions, and if he records them, I take additional notes from the recordings. I do some research for him, and I arrange symposia, like this one. Also, I look after all his travel arrangements, and I take care of all the financial aspects of his research and his job in general."

"Tell me, just briefly, about the rest of the panelists?"

"Okay, another one is Dr. Robin Bobbitt."

She indicated Robin and said, "He's the man with the expensive grey suit and the pale blue shirt with white cuffs and collar. You've probably heard of him? He's the famous TV host of 'Round Pegs, Round Holes?' ... I'm sure you've seen him and heard of him? ..."

She ended each sentence with a bit of an uptick in her voice, as if she was asking a question, just in case Lieutenant Randall hadn't heard of Robin.

"I've heard of him. What about him?"

"He doesn't really have a PhD, not a proper one anyway, but Dr. Melrose got him to agree to be on the panel because he's so well-known and extremely popular. And actually, much of what he says on television does seem to rely on the things that Dr. Melrose teaches and practices. ... taught and practiced."

"How did he and Dr. Melrose get along?"

"I'm not sure. They had some sort of agreement, I think, that Robin would refer patients from his programs to Dr. Melrose, but I don't think Dr. Melrose had much respect for Robin."

"Why not?"

"Robin is a popularizer, not a scholar. He has never done any original research, and his PhD is borderline bogus. Dr. Melrose told me once that the only reason Robin was a hit on television was that the women thought he was good looking."

"What do you think?"

"Well, he *is* devilishly handsome," Phillipa blushed and, knowing she had blushed, she hurried on, "But from what I can tell, his counseling is pretty basic and solid. I think he probably helps quite a few of his callers and on-air guests."

"Who are the other panelists?" asked Lieutenant Randall.

"There's only one other panelist on the schedule ... Dr. Ruth Westover. She's the one walking around over there in the tight skirt, showing cleavage, and flirting with all the men..."

"You disapprove." It came out sounding like a statement, but it was really a question.

"It disgusts me that so many men are beguiled by her superficial attributes and her manner."

Phillipa turned back to Lieutenant Randall and looked him straight in the eye. "The thing is, you see, Ruthie is smart and she's talented, but her flirty manner hides all that."

Repeating the question he had asked her about Robin, Lieutenant Randall asked, "How did she and Dr. Melrose get along?"

"They were 'on again, off again'. Sometimes she was all kissy-huggy with him," Phillipa sneered, "and other times, she was as nasty and negative as I've ever heard anyone be. I think she was trying to use him to get promoted to Full Professor, but he was being coy about it... He certainly wasn't one-hundred percent enthusiastic about supporting her promotion, and that created a lot of tension between them recently."

Lieutenant Randall was interrupted by the arrival of the investigators to help with the questioning, and he broke off his interview with Phillipa to speak with Bob Holly of forensics and Dr. Butts, the Medical Examiner.

He began by telling Bob Holly, "Someone said there was blood on the front edge of the wash basin in the men's room. I sent Officer Keene to find out which men's room it is and to shut it down for now until some of your forensics people can get to it. It's probably the one just straight down the hall from here on the left."

"Yeah, we saw him there on our way here," said Holly. "He looks very official," and he sent two of his forensic specialists to the men's room with a camera and a complete test kit.

"When you're finished there," Holly added to his investigators, "Put up a sign that the restroom is 'out of order', and put up some crime scene tape, just in case we want to get back in there to re-examine anything."

"Better yet," suggested Lieutenant Randall, "Keene is there now keeping people out, so why don't you just keep him there on the door, along with the sign and crime scene tape."

- - -

Dr. Julie Butts was in her early fifties, not quite full-figured, with a head of curly grey-blonde hair. She graduated from The University of Chicago medical school nearly thirty years ago and after being in private general practice for over a decade, she sold her practice to become the Medical Examiner for the county.

"I don't need the hassles of dealing with bills and accounts receivable and office expenses and, mostly, whiny patients," she told everyone who asked ... and many who didn't. "I like being the M.E. – these patients don't whine and don't talk back. And I can earn some pocket change by filling in, doing late shifts in the emergency room now and then when there aren't so many deaths for me to look at."

Another thing Dr. Butts liked about doing Medical-Examiner work was that the patients not only didn't whine, but they didn't wince in pain or complain about anything she did. She could push and poke and shove and cut to her heart's delight.

She wasn't really all that anti-social; in fact, she liked people. It was just that she found doing E.R. and M.E. work meant she wasn't so bothered with the paperwork side of business; and another big plus was that she didn't have to deal with so many repeat visits from hypochondriacs who spent their days searching the internet, looking for new conditions to fret about.

After Dr. Butts spent some time examining the body, Lieutenant Randall asked, "What do you think, Doc?"

He always asked the same question the same way when they were at a potential crime scene together. She hated being called 'Doc', but she had gotten used to it from the lieutenant over the years. He was a quintessential, stereotypical macho male, but she knew he meant 'Doc' as a term of respect; and despite having to put up with all his macho background baggage, she still managed to work well with him on a professional level.

"Judging from his body temperature, he probably died about half an hour ago... certainly, no more than an hour ago ... but I can't give you even a hint about the cause of death. The contusion on his forehead looks serious, but I'm not sure if he suffered a blow serious enough to kill him. The blood around his

21

mouth is a bit of a puzzle. I'll have to 'table' him before I can tell you what killed him."

Dr. Butts hated formal parliamentary procedure, where motions were tabled, and she loved just a hint of saucy irreverence, referring to her examinations of corpses as "tabling the bods."

"What are some likely possibilities?"

"C'mon, Lieutenant, you know the list. Do I really need to go over it for you?"

He nodded, and so she ran through the usual possibilities: "Heart attack, stroke, poison, blow to the head, suffocation, strangulation, stabbing, gunshot, insulin shock – I can't rule out anything at this stage. I don't see any indication of a stabbing or gunshot wound, but who knows what I'll find back at the lab."

"Strangulation? Really? How likely is that?"

"Well, yeah, okay. I can't tell for sure, but there seems to be some bruising or chafing around his neck, and his necktie is outside his collar. That's a possible candidate. Also, there's an interesting little nick on the side of his neck, right at his collar line. When I table the bod, I'll preserve the necktie carefully so Bob Holly can examine any epithelials that might be on it. Be sure to ask about that when you question people. ..."

Lieutenant Randall pretended to be annoyed as part of their give-and-take. He almost whined, "Doc, do I tell you how to do your job?"

Dr. Butts smiled to herself as she tried to ignore the question because, yes, he often *did* tell her how to do her job.

"Well, there may or may not be bruises or other marks around his neck, and so it's hard to tell, but you're right to wonder; strangulation isn't super-likely, but there is no good reason to rule it out, at least not yet. As I said, I can let you know for sure tomorrow after I table him.

"Just so you know, since we can't rule anything out yet, I'll be doing a full tox-screen to check for poisons, and a complete blood work-up to look for anything that can tell us what happened. We'll do a full brain scan to look for blood clots in his brain, and we'll look at his heart, too. He'll get the complete high-roller, penthouse treatment."

She put her hand to her chin. "One other thing, Lieutenant. That tiny nick under his left cheek. It might have been recent, but I'm not sure. So if it was poison... anyway, I'll have to look for recent needle marks or pin pricks. Do you know if he was diabetic or a drug user?"

"I have no idea. I don't see a medic-alert bracelet. I'll check his wallet to see what information is in it, and we'll learn more as the evening goes on. That's a great question, though. Thanks, Doc."

Lieutenant Randall carefully removed Dr. Melrose's wallet from his jacket pocket. A quick glance through it showed credit cards, driver's licence, insurance membership cards, some business cards, and $230 in bills. But no photographs, and no "in case of emergency, please notify..." information. He would have to ask Ms. MaGraw about Dr. Melrose's next of kin when he had a chance. He knew that with this many people in the room, the word would get out soon that Dr. Melrose was dead, and he didn't want the next of kin to learn about it through the media, social or mainstream. He hoped to find some next of kin information so that he could have someone locate them.

Chapter 3 – Suspicious, not definite

It slowly emerged from the early questioning that Dr. Melrose was not particularly well-liked and had lost considerable respect within the profession over the past ten years. The general consensus was that he was arrogant and over-the-hill. He still had enough authority, though, that everyone at the conference felt they had to tolerate him to some extent, especially at this session, which had been heavily billed as his swan song from the ASP. It helped attract an audience that he had insisted on having a temporary bar set up in the conference room and was going to provide some high-end hors d'oeuvres at the end of the evening.

"Cash bar, smash bar," said Roddie Castman, one of the audience members. "Who cares? We're going to have some free hors d'oeuvres! Where else does this happen? We can sit here and drink while the session is going on and then eat afterward! Tell me this ain't great."

After interviewing several people, Sergeant Houston went over to Lieutenant Randall with Patrolman Miller and told him, "Here's something odd that might help, sir. Dr. Melrose went to the men's room about ten minutes before he stumbled back in here; and shortly after he left, four other people left the room, too..." She looked at her notes. "I haven't been able to determine why each of them left, yet, but the four that we've identified so far in our early questioning are MaGraw, Westover, Bobbitt, and Kopfmann, pretty much in that order, at least as far as we can determine."

"Were they the only ones who left the room?" asked Lieutenant Randall.

"So far, yes, that's all we've heard about," answered Patrolman Miller. "They were the only ones out of the room at the same time Dr. Melrose was out; the rest of the audience remained here in this room, mostly chatting and sipping white wine."

Miller did his best to control a sneer about intellectuals sipping white wine.

Sergeant Houston took over again, "But that doesn't rule out the possibility that someone else who isn't here in the room might have killed him. Didn't I read in the paper that there are nearly four hundred people attending this convention? Given what we've heard so far about Dr. Melrose, there must be plenty of people around, here in this room and here in this hotel, who didn't like him."

Lieutenant Randall groaned. "Miller, find the conference organizers and get a list of all the people who are registered for the conference. Get their names, affiliations, addresses, where they are staying while they're here, how they paid their registration fees, and their eye color."

"Eye color?"

"Get used to it, Miller." Sgt Houston chuckled quietly. "That's the lieutenant's idea of a joke."

As Patrolman Miller was leaving the room, he was confronted by members of the media.

"We got a report that there's been a suspicious death here," said Eileen Bosco, beat reporter for the Jericho Journal. She held out her smartphone with the recording app going. "What can you tell us?"

"Me?" asked Miller. "Nothing. Speak with Lieutenant Randall. He's right there at the door," and he scurried off to speak with the hotel management.

Marko Allenson, a local television reporter, immediately moved on and signalled his cameraman to turn on the camera flood light and start the camera rolling.

"Lieutenant Randall," he called "We have a report of a suspicious death here. What can you tell us?"

"Nothing, so far," answered Lieutenant Randall. "We don't even know if it *is* a suspicious death. We have no idea, yet, how the person died."

"Can you at least tell us who the victim is?"

"As I said, we're not even sure it was a suspicious death, and so the word 'victim' might be premature – we're not even sure there *is* a 'victim'. And no, we're not releasing any names until we know more and until we have a chance to notify the next of kin."

Lieutenant Randall had been careful not to use any gendered pronouns in describing the dead person. He saw no reason to give the reporters any idea whether it was a man or a woman, not until he knew more about the dead man himself.

He then went to the other investigators and spoke with them in turn. "During the interviews with these people," he made a sweeping gesture, indicating he meant everyone in the room, "Find out about anyone who isn't here in this room but who might have had a grudge against Dr. Melrose. By 'anyone', I mean anyone who might be here in town at this conference, at the university, or anywhere."

He made his way back to Dr. Melrose's body and stood there, shaking his head, muttering to anyone within earshot, "This is either a neat four-hander or one 'mell of a hess'."

- - -

He turned to Bob Holly, "Well, Bob, what can you tell us so far?"

Holly was in his late thirties, and he had been with forensics for over a decade. He wore rimless glasses, was balding at the temples and at the back of his head, and he always wore the same light green tweed sportcoat. Lieutenant Randall wondered if Holly had several of them in his closet and rotated them.

"Precious little, so far," Holly answered. "It's odd, though, that the victim's necktie is loosened and outside his collar like that. ... That could be important..."

Holly let the word "important" trail off as he paused. He had started to tell Lieutenant Randall, "You should ask everyone about the necktie," but he stopped, knowing that Randall always became irritated and defensive when other people tried to tell him what to do.

"Anything else?" asked Lieutenant Randall.

"I don't know what Butts is going to report," answered Holly, "but if that blow to the head isn't what killed him, and if he wasn't strangled, we'd better start looking for something else. Any suggestions?"

"Heart attack? Stroke? Poison? Suffocation? Those are some of the possibilities the Doc listed. Anything else we should consider?"

Holly was reluctant to suggest anything, but he tentatively added, "Well, on the off chance it was poison, we should be looking for a source. And on the off chance it really was the blow to his head, we should probably be looking for possible blood droplets on the hands or clothing of everyone here, but especially those who might have had the opportunity to hit him or force his head onto the wash basin edge. And, of course, we should be looking for a weapon."

Lieutenant Randall called his investigators over to where he had been talking with Bob Holly. "When we first got here, Sergeant Houston suggested that we search everyone. We still can't tell the cause of death, and so we have to consider natural causes, but we also have to consider poison or a blow to the head or even possibly strangulation or suffocation. So while you're questioning each person, check their hands and clothing for traces of blood. And search their pockets, purses, backpacks, and briefcases to see if there's anything that might have been used to poison him or hit him."

Sergeant Scheffler asked, "Do we know for sure that he was murdered? Or is it possible he really did have a heart attack or a stroke, and he died of natural causes?"

"Good question. The problem is, we don't know. And unfortunately, we won't know until Butts has him up on the table," answered Lieutenant Randall. "But that's going to take her several hours, and right now we don't want to miss anything, so while we have everybody here, let's just treat it as a suspicious death."

"And by the way," he added, "I shouldn't have to say this, but there are media folks out there in the hallway, and until we know anything definite, do **not** speak with them; just refer them to me, no matter what they say or ask. Got that?!"

♂♀

Chapter 4 – **Phillipa**

Phillipa MaGraw grew up in Morkan, Illinois, one of hundreds of small cities in the rust belt in the upper Midwest. The city reached a population of over fifty thousand at its peak in the mid-twentieth century, but through the last few decades, all of its major manufacturing businesses had relocated elsewhere or closed up shop. Its population had shrunk to less than thirty-five thousand, and the town was constantly struggling to reinvent itself, with only limited success.

Phillipa had been a solid student in high school, graduating near the top of her class. She had very little social life then, having gone on some 'desperation dates', as she referred to them, to proms and other special events, but other than those, she didn't date and didn't have many friends that she hung out with. Her dates were with boys who, themselves, didn't date much but felt obliged to have a date for special occasions; she was pleasant and smart, and she was often relied upon by those boys to be available.

Other than academically, Phillipa didn't stand out in any way in high school. She had medium brown hair, grey eyes, and the usual teenage minor acne problems. She dressed somewhat conservatively and inexpensively – not at the cutting edge of fashion but also not obviously wearing things from Goodwill that were years out of date.

In truth, Phillipa wasn't at all unattractive, but she was never thought of as attractive, either. She was unimposing, unimpressive, and just there ... one of the many students in her school. She was pleasant to other students, but she was quiet and rarely spoke out in social settings or in her classes.

That same pattern followed her when she enrolled as an undergraduate at Jericho State University. She was pleasant and quiet, both socially and in the classroom. She dated, albeit rarely, but again she was mostly just there.

She had often been told that she had a 'great body'. She didn't see it that way, though; she thought of herself as maybe slim and fit, but mostly skinny. During her sophomore year at Jericho State, she decided to lose her virginity, not out of love or anything remotely resembling love, but because she wanted to experience sex and she wanted to feel desired. It was a one-night stand with a student from the chemistry department, whom she never saw again, which suited her just fine.

Also during her sophomore year, Phillipa decided to major in psychology. That year and the next, in addition to enrolling in a few psychology courses, she took a smattering of other courses in sociology, social work, and organizational management. And to satisfy the diversification requirements, she took the 'baby' courses in statistics, geology, and history – introductory courses for non-majors. She had no idea what she wanted to do after graduation, but she pretty much assumed she would become a teacher or maybe a social worker or counsellor of some flavor.

In her senior year, Phillipa took almost exclusively psychology courses. During the fall term she had a course in abnormal psychology with Dr. Melrose and became enthralled with him, his ideas, and his lecture style. She hung on his every word in class, and as the term progressed she began arriving at class early to make sure she could get a front row seat. She dominated the class on the midterm and final exams... seriously dominated it. Her answers to the exam questions were so good that Dr. Melrose had to admit they were probably more complete and better than he would have written himself. He even photocopied her final exam answers to keep in his files.

In the last term of her senior year, she switched from a rat-maze-lab course on learning theory to a small honors seminar in Freudian analysis that Dr. Melrose led. She hadn't signed up for the seminar during fall registration, but after having had one course with him, she wanted another.

Phillipa wouldn't ordinarily have taken a seminar; she was a little shy, and she didn't want to be put on the spot, having to answer questions and discuss ideas. Besides, she didn't see that there was any great reason to study Freudian analysis since, according to most of her other professors, it was passé at best. However, since Dr. Melrose was teaching the course...

In the early weeks of the seminar, it became clear that Dr. Melrose was focusing much of his attention on her and her ideas. She was flattered that he seemed to recognize and respect her abilities as a student, and so she worked especially hard, preparing for each week's meeting of the seminar, not just keeping up with the assigned reading but also searching out other material she thought might be relevant. During the second half of the term, she even started visiting Dr. Melrose during his office hours to discuss various topics that piqued her interest.

A few weeks before the term ended, Dr. Melrose called her into his office. "Phillipa, you've been an exemplary student. I have a research grant, and I would love to have you working on it with me. Would you like to work for me this summer?"

Phillipa was overcome with joy and excitement. She couldn't think of anything she would rather do. She loved reading, studying, and researching Freudian theories, and she was finding herself quite in awe of Dr. Melrose as well. She'd been planning to go back to her hometown of Morkan and bide her time while she tried to decide what to do next, but the summer job offer from Dr. Melrose was perfect for her.

A month into the summer, he asked her to come into his office for a few minutes. After she sat down across the desk from him, he told her, "This research grant runs out at the end of this summer..."

Phillipa's heart sank.

"... but I always have several other research grants on the go. Why don't you stay here, working with me as my full-time, permanent assistant?"

She jumped up, ran around the desk, and threw her arms around him, saying, "You have no idea how happy this makes me!"

They went out for a celebratory drink that evening and ended up in bed together that night at her apartment.

Phillipa had no illusions about her illusions. She knew that what she felt for Dr. Melrose was more akin to idolatry than caring or loving. But she didn't care. She had a job with, and had slept with, a man she practically worshipped.

As the years went by, Phillipa progressed from being a citation-checking research assistant to becoming an overall assistant in every area of Dr. Melrose's academic and professional life. Phillipa worked hard, and she carefully controlled Dr. Melrose in ways that helped him avoid major gaffs in his therapy sessions, his writing, and his life overall. Eventually, she had her own office at Jericho State University and fronted for Dr. Melrose in many different ways. He even began to include her name as a co-author on some of his published journal articles. She had become indispensable to him. After eight years, he convinced the psychology department and the university to convert her position to a regular, level four, university administrative position with a pay raise and full benefits.

Meanwhile, though, her relationship with Dr. Melrose wasn't entirely satisfactory. Early on, he said to her, "My dear, I'm more than twenty years older than you are. I wouldn't want to saddle you with an old man in your life, so let's just enjoy getting together every once in a while."

Phillipa was over her idol-worship by the time he told her that. But she still loved being associated with him and almost being his partner academically, if not romantically. She knew he didn't treat her with the respect she deserved, and she knew he tried to bed nearly every female he met. She suspected that he even slept with some of his patients, seriously violating the ethics of his profession. She didn't want to know for sure, though.

He paid her well, and she was happy to be doing work she enjoyed. She was still active in the realm of Freudian psychology, learning and contributing to the work of Dr. Melrose. But more than that, she had more power and authority than she had ever had in her life, and she had earned considerable respect from all the faculty members in the psychology department at Jericho State. It was okay with her if all Dr. Melrose did was take her out for a drink and to bed every once in a while, usually whenever he couldn't seduce anyone else.

☌

Chapter 5 -- Andrew

Six years after Phillipa began working for Dr. Melrose, Andrew Kopfmann accepted a fellowship to do graduate studies with Dr. Melrose at Jericho State. Phillipa was twenty-seven, and Andrew was twenty-six.

Phillipa was attracted to Andy from the day he arrived, and her attraction to him never waned. She frequently did little things to ingratiate herself with him: she smiled at him, she plotted to sit next to him in pubs when the graduate students went out for drinks, and she helped him complete the paperwork for grants to help cover his research and travel expenses.

She carefully avoided fawning over Andy overtly, though, and she was especially careful not to seem too taken with him when Dr. Melrose was around because she knew it would upset him. Somehow, Dr. Melrose had conveyed a clear message to her that although he, himself, wasn't tied down to her in a relationship, implicitly she was tied down to him, and she should not get involved with anyone else, especially not a student, unless she had a new job lined up for herself. He never said so much, at least not in those words, but it was a strong sense she had. She knew it wasn't right, but she also liked her job and she didn't have any idea what she would do for work if she lost her job with Dr. Melrose. It was the only job she had ever known, and the fact was that she loved the job and still enjoyed many aspects of her relationship with Dr. Melrose.

Despite all her efforts to interest Andy, he treated her merely as a pleasant, helpful administrative assistant. For sure, he was grateful for all the things she did to make his life in graduate school go more smoothly, but he never felt or showed any kind of physical or romantic interest in her. In fact, he barely acknowledged her existence most of the time.

- - -

Andy Kopfmann was born in Nanaimo, British Columbia, on Vancouver Island, across the strait from the city of Vancouver. The fourth of four children, he had been a gregarious, friendly person all through school.

He had a strange lock of white hair on the left side near the back of his head that stood out in contrast from the rest of his medium brown hair. It was always there; it grew that way as his blonde hair turned darker when he was a child. He never thought much about it, except he knew it made him look 'interesting' or, as his mother had said, 'distinguished'. Other than that lock of white hair, though, he was pretty standard-looking: five foot eleven, normal weight and shape, brown eyes, oval face and a big smile with perfect teeth.

Andy did his undergraduate studies at U-Vic – the University of Victoria on Vancouver Island – followed by a master's degree in psychology at Simon Fraser

University up on a mountain outside Vancouver. All through high school and university, Andy had been popular and had had numerous close relationships with different women, usually those he met in his classes. When the relationships ended, he remained good friends with them. That only seemed natural to him.

While he was completing a master's degree, his faculty advisors strongly urged Andy to apply for admission and fellowships for doctoral programs at some of the major universities in the United States. He followed their advice, and Jericho State University offered what he thought was the best overall package: a fellowship, a guarantee of additional summer research assistance money working for Dr. Melrose, and a tuition waiver. He knew that working with Dr. Melrose would open a lot of doors for him professionally, and so he eagerly accepted that position.

During his second year in graduate school, Andy became fascinated by some Freudian theories of group dynamics. Dr. Melrose had touched on them somewhat in his own research, and Andy believed he could make additional contributions to the field by studying group dynamics in conflicting cultures. To carry out his research, he secured funding to spend six months working with both the Hutu and Tutsi tribes in Rwanda. Unfortunately for Andy, however, the continued political strife in Rwanda forced him to cut short his research there.

"Are you sure you can't use the information you have already collected?" asked Dr. Melrose. "Maybe flesh it out a bit somehow...?"

Andy seriously doubted whether he could get such scant research past an examining committee for a PhD, and he wondered if Dr. Melrose was suggesting that the two of them should work together to write up studies based on what he *expected* to find and based on the theories of Dr. Melrose, rather than based on actual field studies. The trouble with that plan was that anything they wrote up would only be speculative and not really based on much field research.

Instead, he said "I think I can use the material I gathered in Rwanda as a portion of my doctoral dissertation, but there really isn't enough there for a full PhD dissertation; at least I wouldn't want to try to get it past the examination board."

Andy felt lost. He had no direction, not even a vague sense of a plan, and so he applied for and received a one-year leave from his fellowship and from his graduate studies. To collect his thoughts, Andy returned to Vancouver, where he had friends and family that he could count on for both emotional and financial support. He continued his reading and thinking about group dynamics, and he took odd jobs in various restaurants to support himself during the hiatus from his graduate work. He took delight in sometimes wearing a T-shirt that said, "You're a grad student? Which restaurant?"

While he was in Vancouver, he began to realize that the Bunu gangs there and in Vietnam had some interesting similarities as well as some fascinating differences, and he could continue his research on group dynamics in similar but conflicting cultures by working with those gangs and studying them. With the assistance of Phillipa and Dr. Melrose, he applied successfully for additional financial assistance to travel between Vancouver and Vietnam to carry out extensive field studies.

When he finished his research in Vietnam and Vancouver, he returned to graduate school at Jericho State for his last year, where he spent countless hours in the library and in his cubbyhole office out in the eaves of the attic at Guthrie Hall, reading more about group dynamics and writing up his research results.

His work was good enough not only to earn him a PhD but also to win some minor acclaim for his creative incorporation of primal scream therapy with Freudian concepts of the id and the ego, thus forming the basis of his own, unique analysis of group dynamics.

Andy was happy with the results of his research, and he was even happier with his inner renewal – he had regained his confidence, and he felt re-energized. With his PhD in hand and some interesting research results, he was offered several attractive jobs, but he chose to accept a position offered by the Vancouver Academy of Global Studies because it was in a geographic area that he had come to think of as home; but the job also appealed to him because it involved roughly half research and half clinical work, continuing his involvement with street gangs.

The one thing that bothered Andy on the research side of his career was that Dr. Melrose consistently reinterpreted Andy's research so that it was consistent with what he called, 'my seminal findings,' referring to his publications from thirty years earlier. Andy didn't think his work was as supportive as Dr. Melrose made it out to seem, and he resented Dr. Melrose's continued misrepresentation of his work.

He felt as if Dr. Melrose was trying to hijack his results and in the process was harming Andy's career and reputation.

- - -

During Andy's final year on campus, Phillipa persisted with her attempts to attract his interest. Her only progress was that Andy now treated her more as a good friend and less as merely a very helpful administrative assistant.

But it never got any farther than that, and one reason it didn't was that while Andy was away, the university hired Ruthie Westover. When Andy met her upon his return, he was hopelessly smitten with her.

☿♀

Chapter 6 – Ruthie

Ruthie Westover had led an "interesting" life, growing up in Brazil, Indiana, just an hour west of Indianapolis. Her mother was an exotic dancer who traveled around the country performing strip shows in bars and clubs of varying degrees of sleaze. When the men watching her were worked up enough, she prostituted herself.

Ruthie's father was an insipid car salesman. He didn't have great charm, and he wasn't particularly pushy or aggressive, and so he just coasted along in his job, selling enough cars to earn a bit of a living, but also drinking too much after work and relying on his wife's income without asking very many questions about where it came from.

They led quite separate lives.

When Ruthie was in eighth grade, she had an affair with Mr. O'Brien, her good-looking, twenty-four-year-old math teacher. She learned from that experience that she could flatter men and use sex to get almost anything she wanted, and over the next three years she refined those skills and talents carefully. She read all the pornography she could find, trying to improve her style, approaches, and techniques.

In the early winter of her junior year in high school, she spent an entire weekend drinking and having sex with the varsity basketball team. It had been what she had thought of as fun, but she felt empty afterward, and over the next few days she made a life-changing transformation. She looked at her own life and then at her mother's life and asked herself, "Is that really how I want to end up?"

Her answer was that she didn't. She wanted more... more pay, more job security, more prestige, more respect, and more class. She realized she would have to think about her life with a longer-term perspective than her mother ever had.

After her 'basketball-team weekend', Ruthie stopped going out every weekend, partying, and drinking. Instead, she cultivated new friendships with different classmates, both male and female, who had more sophisticated backgrounds than hers and who had higher aspirations for themselves. She buckled down in school and earned good grades by actually studying instead of using her body. She even joined the Junior Red Cross and helped put on programs for children at the local orphanage.

Flirting and using her flirtatious manner to influence both her teachers and her classmates had become habitual, though, with the result that many of the girls in her classes still resented her. Nevertheless, she worked hard to become sincere (or to at least try to look as if she was sincere) when she was with them.

Much to Ruthie's delight, her changes paid off in several ways. She became more popular with all the students, not just the drinker-partiers. More importantly she did well on her SATs, got good grades, and won a scholarship to Miami University in Oxford, Ohio.

Ruthie excelled in the university setting and after her studies at Miami, she was offered a full-ride fellowship including a substantial stipend to do graduate work in psychology at Tulane University in New Orleans. She loved New Orleans, especially the night life; and she also enjoyed her graduate studies, specializing in the psychology of sex, to the surprise of no one who knew her at all well.

When she finished her PhD, Ruthie looked for a job that would pay well, allow her time for a part-time private therapy practice, and offer some long-term job security. She had several options, but she accepted the job offer from Jericho State University; the pay was good, and they had a standing policy that members of the psychology department could spend up to twenty hours a week doing private counseling, with everyone assuring her that no one would care if she actually shaded that up above twenty hours in some weeks. She was also attracted to the job at Jericho State because during the interview process, it became quite obvious to her that she could use her personal attractions to manipulate Dr. Melrose. He was an important figure in the field of Freudian analysis, and she planned to use her association with him to further her career as she moved on to bigger and better things over the next five or ten years.

During her first year on the job, she was promoted from Lecturer to Assistant Professor. And four years later, Ruthie was offered early promotion to the rank of Associate Professor with tenure. More recently, she had begun lobbying for a promotion to Full Professor, and she had her eye on an endowed chair in the department – but she hadn't yet been successful in reaching those goals.

A major obstacle to her being promoted further was that her research, while interesting, had not been particularly rigorous and had appeared only in minor, less impressive psychology journals. No matter what her personal talents were, and no matter how she employed them in the department, she needed a more substantial research record to justify another promotion.

It didn't help matters that even though Ruthie and Dr. Melrose usually got along well, in every sense of the phrase, her conclusions from her research were at variance with the conclusions Dr. Melrose had reached thirty years earlier, when he was at the top of his field. Initially, Ruthie didn't understand the strength of Dr. Melrose's ego and his attachment to his own work, but when she did, she explained to him, "I'm just extending your work, James, I'm building on it as we explore more about the psychology of sex. I'm not challenging your findings at all, not in any way; I'm treating them as foundational."

It was a good line to use with Dr. Melrose. He was flattered by her treatment of his work as 'foundational'. At the same time, she had sex with him just frequently enough to keep him flattered in other ways as well.

Meanwhile, Ruthie built up a thriving private practice involving a mish-mash of *The Joy of Sex*, Freudian analysis, and some physical group work with clients who, according to her, wanted and needed to explore beyond their straight-laced Victorian upbringings.

There were rumors that she had sex with her clients as part of their therapy and was little more than a high-class call girl, but the rumors were never substantiated.

Early in her career at Jericho State University, Ruthie and Andy Kopfmann had a brief fling. Well... it was a brief fling for her, but Andy was completely bewitched by her. He kept pestering her, wanting to sleep with her again, wanting to go out with her, and probably, in his own fantasies, wanting to marry her.

Ruthie tried to make it clear from the beginning that she liked Andy and that she had enjoyed their fling, but what they did, what they had done, and what they were to each other was never going to amount to more than having had a brief fling. She was polite, even cordial, with him, especially in public. In private, she was more definite:

"It ain't happenin', Andy. It was a nice time, but move on. I think Phillipa might be a lot more interested than I am..."

⚥

Chapter 7 – **Robin**

Early in Ruthie's career, one of her many partners was Robin Bobbitt, who began studying for a master's degree in psychology at Jericho State five years after Ruthie was hired. He had passed Ruthie in the hallway of Guthrie Hall, where the psychology department had its offices, but she looked so young he assumed she was a fellow graduate student. He couldn't believe someone who looked that young and who was that attractive was actually a faculty member – a faculty member who, no less, had been there long enough to have been promoted with tenure! Fortunately, he kept those thoughts to himself as he began to chat with her now and then.

He was attracted to her. She had a great smile and long dark hair; and she wore her glasses on top of her head most of the time. Like most women, she found Robin very attractive, both in his looks and in his calm, interested and caring manner. Moreover, she found him 'interesting'. Their courtship was intense as they explored each other's minds and bodies in both standard and unusual ways. They met for lunch, they met for drinks before dinner, and they had dinner together occasionally.

During their courtship, they spent only one or two nights together each week. "I have clients to meet, research proposals to write, and other work to get done, too," said Ruthie. "I can't spend all my time with you, Robbie."

"And," she continued, "you need to study! You have good insights, but you're not going to make it in grad school if you don't buckle down."

Ruthie was right. After two years in the master's program, Robin was given what everyone regarded as a consolation master's degree, a degree that in essence said to the student (and nearly everyone else), "You passed your courses and wrote a barely acceptable master's research paper, but you clearly don't have what it takes to do a PhD. Congratulations and best wishes for the future. Thank you. Now please go away."

- - -

Robin had been raised by an upper-middle-class family in the upper-class suburb of Rye, New York, where he and his older brother, Arthur, enjoyed their picture-perfect suburban life with their parents. After high school, Robin went to Cornell University where he was so popular that he even managed to beat out some of the star athletes to win the election for Prom King in his senior year.

Academically at Cornell, Robin did acceptably well, but he wasn't *Phi Beta Kappa* material, not by any stretch of the imagination. He drifted from major to major and finally graduated with a degree in 'distributed studies', which was another way of saying he had no major.

"That's okay," he told everyone. "I'd rather be well-rounded than specialize too much in anything."

After graduation, Robin sold cars for a year, sold life insurance for two years, and sold real estate for another two years. He earned a living in sales, in large measure because of his looks and his winning personality. But he was unhappy with the jobs.

"I don't see myself doing this for the rest of my life," he told Arthur, his older brother.

"What **would** you like to do, then?" asked Arthur.

"I'd be a good therapist. I want to go to graduate school in psychology."

He applied to at least fifteen different graduate schools in psychology, but because of his time off from college and because his grades didn't put him in the top ten percent of graduates from Cornell, he wasn't admitted to most of the programs. A few of the lesser programs admitted him but with no financial aid of any kind, not even a tuition waiver.

He knew what he wanted, though, and in desperation he began a tour, visiting several different graduate schools, hoping that he could use his winning ways to gain admission with some sort of financial aid.

Before traveling to Jericho State University, Robin read several articles about Dr. Melrose and read some of his research papers. He arranged to spend some time with Dr. Melrose during the visit and flattered Dr. Melrose by discussing his major papers with him, challenging him a bit, but always asking for explanations and help in understanding what Dr. Melrose meant.

It worked. Dr. Melrose made sure Robin was admitted with full financial aid, and when he struggled in his first year in the program, Dr. Melrose defended him, saying, "He's a bright man. He's been out of school for quite a few years. Mark my words, he'll be a success eventually."

Because of Dr. Melrose's insistence, the other faculty members allowed Robin to continue in the graduate program, but on probation. The probation basically meant he'd be allowed to continue studying at the master's degree level, but if he didn't show more promise, he would not be allowed to go on into the doctoral program.

With Ruthie's help, he managed to write an acceptable master's paper on "Active Listening in a Vengeful Relationship," and was awarded the consolation master's degree in psychology.

Robin knew what his degree meant, but he didn't care: he had an advanced degree in psychology that he soon parlayed into a very successful radio and television career. People called him with their problems, and he would make them feel better. His basic approach was an old standard: be positive and help the callers think positively and constructively about their lives. He called his program "Round Pegs, Round Holes" to emphasize his approach.

"There's a place for everyone in this world," he told his audiences, "including a place just for you. It won't appear by magic, though. You have to look for it, you have to work for it, and you have to recognize it when you find it. Don't try to fit a square peg in a round hole," he said. "Find your place and work to understand it."

Robin's place was in the media. He loved the limelight, and he dealt with callers in a kind and caring, yet honest way. It helped his television ratings that he was very good-looking.

After just a few months of successful media work, his programs went into syndication and were carried all across North America, with some links around the world as well. Based mostly on his popularity but also on his work with the show's callers, a university called *York of Yakima* in Yakima, Washington, got in touch with him. They wanted to claim him as an alumnus, and so they offered him a PhD based almost entirely on his on-air clinical work.

"Just send us a 50-to-60-page summary of what you do and why you do it, and we'll grant you a PhD."

Robin got the distinct impression they didn't care what he wrote or, for that matter, if he even wrote it himself. They hadn't said "write up and send us"; they had said "send us".

Robin hesitated for a few weeks, but the idea of being able to call himself "Dr. Robin Bobbitt" appealed to him, and so he accepted their offer. As he began writing up the required document for *York of Yakima*, he began to feel increasingly pleased with himself. He saw that he had accomplished a great deal and had helped a lot of people along the way. Also, having to write up his experiences helped him gain a better understanding of what he did, what had made him successful, and why he approached media therapy the way he did.

York of Yakima invited him to give the commencement address that year and conferred on him not only his barely legitimate PhD in Psychology but also an honorary Doctor of Laws. In return, he made a sizable donation to the university, as everyone silently expected. It was an unacknowledged trade: He received a nearly legitimate doctorate and an honorary degree, and in exchange they got both his money and his name as an alumnus.

Robin had been glad to leave academia. He didn't want to teach or do research; he wanted to do counseling. Also, he was happy to get away from seeing Ruthie every day. She ended their relationship right after he finished his master's paper and after they had been together for nearly a year and a half.

He hated even passing Ruthie in the hallway. They tried to be cordial with each other, but he had considerable resentment about her having rejected him after their intense relationship. He understood the resentment he felt; he even understood enough about himself to know why he was holding onto that resentment. But the resentment still managed to seep out whenever Ruthie was around. They tried to keep things on a friendly level, but they often ended up sparring or sniping at each other because his underlying feelings brought out the worst in her. She didn't have those feelings of resentment herself, but she resented his feelings of resentment, and the clashing resentments made situations awkward for them both while he was still on campus at Jericho State. He was more-than-comfortable leaving Jericho State and having Ruthie out of his life.

- - -

Two years ago, Phillipa MaGraw called Robin. Dr. Melrose wanted to meet with him to discuss a possibly mutually beneficial arrangement. Robin had been approached by many people who wanted to ride along on his popular, media-driven coattails or use his name in some way, but he couldn't imagine what Dr. Melrose wanted. Because Robin respected Dr. Melrose and was grateful for all the support Dr. Melrose had given him – getting him into graduate school and keeping him there for the second year so he could receive his master's degree, he felt he owed it to Dr. Melrose to meet with him; besides he was curious.

Over lunch, Dr. Melrose laid out his plan: if there wasn't enough time for Robin to deal with all his callers, Robin should refer patients in the Jericho region to him. He would reciprocate with referral fees and invitations to various academic events that would add to Robin's academic credentials.

Robin received hundreds more inquiries and pleas for counseling each week than he could deal with on the air, and he had been approached about referrals by innumerable therapists and counselors. He politely declined nearly all the offers or requests for collaboration, but the offer from Dr. Melrose, with its attendant academic panache, appealed to him. They worked out an arrangement, and, true to his word, Dr. Melrose made sure that 'Dr. Robin Bobbitt' was included as a highlighted panel member at several academic conferences.

One problem with the arrangement, though, was that Dr. Melrose was **not** true to his word about paying referral fees. He gladly accepted patients referred to him by Robin for his private practice, but he neglected to pay Robin anything.

Robin called Phillipa a few times to inquire about the fees, and she said she would make sure Dr. Melrose got back to him about them. He never did get back to Robin, though. In fact, he was quite bothered anytime Phillipa mentioned the calls or the referral fees.

"I don't owe him any referral fees," he said. "Most of the patients he referred to me never bothered to make appointments, and of those that did, most discontinued their sessions after only one or two visits."

Phillipa didn't know the details of the agreement between Dr. Melrose and Robin, but she suspected that Dr. Melrose was making quite a bit of money from the patients Robin sent his way; however, her loyalty to Dr. Melrose prevented her from saying anything about the patients or the fees to Robin. Whenever Robin called her, she feigned ignorance and said, "I'll make sure Dr. Melrose gets this message and looks into the situation. I'm sure he won't let it slip by this time."

- - -

At one point during the social mingling before that evening's session was to begin, Robin confronted Dr. Melrose about the referral fees. Their exchange was loud enough for more than just a few people to hear and later relate to Lieutenant Randall and the investigators.

"James, I need to talk with you," said Robin.

55

"Not here. This is not the time ..."

"This most definitely **is** the time, and here is as good a place as any. By my count, I have sent fifty-nine patients your way over the past eighteen months, and the promised referral fees have not been forthcoming. I don't know how long each of those fifty-nine patients stuck with you, but my rough estimate is that you owe me at least five thousand dollars in referral fees!"

"Why didn't you raise this with me earlier at dinner, Robin? Anyway, I'm sure you are doing well enough with your media work that you don't need a paltry few thousand dollars or whatever it is you say I owe you..."

Robin began to fume. He had tried to raise the question at dinner but had been put off by Dr. Melrose.

"Besides," added Dr. Melrose, "most of the patients you referred to me didn't even book one session with me, and of those that did, most of them didn't return. I don't owe you for any of those referrals. I'll send you a check for $300 for those who did stay with me. Phillipa..."

Dr. Melrose was about to ask Phillipa to look after writing the check for him.

"That's outrageous," Robin interrupted in a loud voice. "You know very well that we agreed you would pay me for every single referral and that you would pay me even more for those who saw you for more than two sessions. And don't blame me if your style wasn't good enough to keep them coming back. Just how much money did you make from those referrals, anyway?"

"I'll send you $300," Dr. Melrose repeated, "and not a penny more. ... No, on second thought, I'll make it one penny more. I'll send you a check for three hundred dollars and one cent."

Dr. Melrose continued, "Do you have any proof we made such an agreement? If you do, sue me."

"You know I have no proof. I trusted you. It was a gentlemen's handshake."

"I repeat, so sue me," said Dr. Melrose as he turned away.

Robin knew that Dr. Melrose had the upper hand in the dispute because Robin had no intention of suing him, not even in small-claims court. If it got out that he was collecting referral fees, some viewers and some media pundits would make it look as if he was getting kickbacks and bribes from Dr. Melrose, as well as others to whom he was referring patients. He couldn't really afford to look greedy; it would undoubtedly hurt his ratings.

Robin was livid. He knew he didn't need the money, and yet it galled him that Dr. Melrose had abused his trust. He couldn't let him get by with such an affront; now that Dr. Melrose had publicly rebuked and embarrassed him, Robin felt as if he would have to do something to put Dr. Melrose in his place. He had already decided that if Dr. Melrose didn't pay up, he would stop sending him patients. Maybe he'd even rekindle something with Ruthie and send them to her...

Meanwhile, he had to think of some way to deal with or, in truth, get even with, Dr. Melrose.

Chapter 8 -- Disruption

Dr. Melrose's session at the ASP convention was supposed to open with a cash wine-and-beer bar and some social mingling. It got off to a bad start, though.

After most of the audience members had arrived and were milling around, buying drinks, and waiting for the session to begin, they were surprised to hear Phillipa screaming out in the hallway.

"WHAT??? How could you be so incompetent??!!

She burst into the room and called out, "Dr. Melrose, I'm sorry, but the staff at this hotel have completely fouled up the arrangements for the computer-video equipment for your session this evening."

"Phillipa, you should have been on top of this situation; you should have confirmed all of the arrangements in advance. How could you let this happen?"

Phillipa bristled.

"I *did* confirm everything, Dr. Melrose!" She was furious. It was almost as if she was stamping her foot as she continued, "I confirmed the arrangements yesterday, and I reconfirmed them right after lunch today. Those idiots say they accidentally switched the room names in the file with the equipment repair requisitions."

"We need that video equipment," Dr. Melrose said, in measured tones. "Several of us will want to use it for our power-point presentations."

Andy Kopfmann interjected, "I don't know about the others, Dr. Melrose, but if it will help make things easier for everyone, I'm sure I can do my presentation, with just a white board on an easel along with some markers ..."

Phillipa almost swooned, assuming that Andy was trying to help her out. She smiled at him saying, "Thanks, Andy..."

But Dr. Melrose cut her off, "Thank you, Dr. Kopfmann..." He said in very measured tones. He clearly was upset, for if he hadn't been upset, he'd have called him 'Andy'.

The session was supposed to be in his honor, and he wanted everything to be perfect. He didn't welcome the confusion about the video equipment, nor did he welcome Andy's offer to go ahead without the equipment. Not having the equipment would lessen the impact of his own concluding presentation and would make Dr. Kopfmann's presentation on a whiteboard, if it came to that, look like a cheap sideshow.

He continued to Andy, "I know that your power-point slides will be much more impressive than hand-drawn replicas on a whiteboard. And, of course, I am counting on having the video equipment for my own presentation as well."

"Phillipa," he added, "Go get this taken care of immediately."

She turned to leave the room, fuming.

As she was going out the door, Dr. Melrose continued to Andy, "We need to be able to present those slides of yours, Dr. Kopfmann, so we can clarify the connection between my own, original path-breaking work and your extensions to make the linkages as strong as possible."

Before anyone else could add anything, Ruthie Westover shouted out, "Which path-breaking work of yours are you referring to, James? Is it your famous study of 'Sex in the Lizard Colony', published thirty-three years ago? Or is it your classic, 'Freudian Insights into Open-Heart Surgery', published only thirty-one years ago?"

Melrose glared at Ruthie and as he was about to respond, Phillipa was back in the room with her cellphone, speaking loudly so that everyone could hear her, "That's right. We need that equipment immediately for Dr. Melrose's panel. ... We're in the..." she stepped back out of the room to look at the name on the door, "Lincoln Room..."

"I don't care if the equipment *is* in another room where there's a different panel in session, get it now! ... . Well, of course you'll have to inconvenience them by interrupting their session, but that will be for only a few minutes. Meanwhile you want to inconvenience our entire session by making us wait for an hour?! You screwed it up, so you fix it! Now!"

Andy looked at her in surprise. This was a side of Phillipa that he hadn't seen before. She had always seemed well-organized and in control of details, and she had always seemed polite and calm; he had never seen this angry, bossy, brash domineering side of her.

"Have it here in half an hour," she shouted into the phone. "Or less!" and she hung up, punching "OFF" on her cell phone in anger.

After the hubbub died down, Dr. Melrose turned to the others in the room and said, "As you all heard, it will apparently be another half hour or so before we can begin the formal presentations for this session of the conference. In the meantime, why don't I introduce and say a few words about each of our panelists...

⚦

Chapter 9 -- **Introductions**

Phillipa quietly slid alongside Dr. Melrose and murmured a reminder to him, "Remember, be nice."

He nodded distractedly, but she had no idea what that would mean when he began speaking. He had a tendency to make negative comments to and about nearly everyone, claiming all the while that he was joking.

When people told him they were offended by his biting comments, his pat reply was always, "I like you! Otherwise I wouldn't joke with you like this. If I didn't like you, I wouldn't feel free to joke this way."

The problem, though, was that everyone knew he wasn't joking; he really meant the nasty things he said as he smiled and pretended to be joking.

- - -

Dr. Melrose addressed the group, "Ladies, gentlemen, and fellow ASPs."

He paused and smiled at his old, stale joke that nearly every member of ASP had made more than a dozen times in their own careers.

"I'm glad you could be here with me this evening. We have a superb panel of scholars who will be speaking at this evening's session. As you can see, the bar is open now and will stay open throughout the presentations and discussions. And when the session concludes, the bar will remain open, and we will also be providing some hors d'oeuvres, courtesy of The Melrose Program at Jericho State University, in co-operation with the SGA Foundation.

"While we are waiting for the hotel I-T staff to bring in the computer and video equipment and set it up, perhaps you could all find a seat, and I'll introduce each of the panelists for this evening's session."

After a few moments, everyone who wasn't waiting for a drink at the bar had found a seat, and Dr. Melrose continued.

"Our first presenter will be Dr. Andrew Kopfmann. Dr. Kopfmann is here, courtesy of a special grant I was able to secure from the SGA Foundation to cover his travel expenses to fly all the way here from Liechtenstein, where he has been seconded from his home institution in Vancouver to work on a special project involving group dynamics between people living in a small sovereignty but interacting constantly with residents of the larger collective, the Eurozone. Dr. Kopfmann's home institution is the Vancouver Academy of Global Studies, where he has made quite a name for himself, studying group dynamics in the Bunu gangs, which are strong in both Vancouver and Vietnam.

Dr. Kopfmann was raised in British Columbia, and he studied at The University of Victoria and Simon Fraser University before doing his PhD under my supervision, here at Jericho State University.

"Dr. Kopfmann's theories are that the members of the gangs tend to exhibit numerous identifiable Freudian characteristics. Some have joined the gangs because of a fear of rejection at home... there's a sense of an Oedipal complex emerging in many of those findings. Others have joined the gangs out of pure penis envy, hoping to enhance the masculine sides of their personalities by becoming enforcers within the gangs. Still others..."

Andy ducked his head and coughed noticeably. Then he looked at Ruthie, whom he had schemed to end up standing next to, and under his breath he whispered, "Is he going to leave anything for me to present?"

"But I'm getting ahead of things," Dr. Melrose continued in a very patronizing tone, "I really must leave it to Dr. Kopfmann to explain his theories. He will do a much better job than I could ever hope to do.

"There is one major point that requires emphasizing, however, and I am bringing this out now because I'm sure Dr. Kopfmann is too modest to mention it himself. This point is that his research into group dynamics has really pushed the science ahead by leaps and bounds; and he got to this point because of his reliance on the Freudian underpinnings he learned while he was studying with me in graduate school here at Jericho State.

"Ladies and gentlemen, Andrew Kopfmann," and as he gestured toward Andy, Phillipa led the applause, almost as if on cue.

When the applause had died down, Andy surprised Dr. Melrose by addressing the room. "Thank you, Dr. Melrose. If I might just briefly foreshadow what I'll be saying later, there are developments in my research which quite clearly distinguish it from the work you did way back then."

And before Dr. Melrose could interrupt him, Andy added, "The discussion portion of tonight's session should be very lively..."

"Yes, yes," Dr. Melrose managed to interject. "We are all looking forward to it, I'm sure."

Dr. Melrose quickly continued, "Our second panelist this evening is *Doctor* Robin Bobbitt, the well-known host of the radio and television counselling programs, 'Round Pegs, Round Holes', a **very** Freudian title if I ever heard one," and again he chuckled at his own joke.

"As some of you may know, *Doctor* Bobbitt is yet another former student in the long list of world-renowned experts who studied with me at Jericho State University. However, *Doctor* Bobbitt's career took a somewhat different path than might ordinarily have been expected from one of my graduates.

"After studying with me for two years, Dr. Bobbitt was given a masters' degree. But he didn't stop there. He went on to become the well-known media host he is today, winning both acclaim and large followings because of his adroit use of what he learned from us. Some years later, based on his media counselling work, York University of Yakima granted him a doctor's degree, even though he never actually studied there. That's how impressive his work has been!

"But of course that doesn't matter. Dr. Bobbitt doesn't really need any credentials. He is clearly doing very well and is very successful with his on-air counselling. And we will certainly enjoy listening to his presentation later this evening."

He paused significantly, and once again Phillipa felt obliged to start some applause.

Robin was used to Dr. Melrose's back-handed compliments that were more like jabs and insults than compliments. He spoke out briefly, "Thank you James. And I hope you're grateful that all my own personal success means more referrals to you and your own private practice..."

Robin's response was designed to embarrass Dr. Melrose. It made Robin look superior to Dr. Melrose, as if Robin was throwing some crumbs to him. Furthermore, people didn't openly discuss referrals and referral fees, and Robin knew that making an explicit reference to the referrals would raise some interesting questions about Dr. Melrose's private practice. By mentioning the referrals publicly, Robin hoped he was putting additional pressure on Dr. Melrose to pay him the full amount of referral fees to which they had agreed. But mostly he wanted to one-up and embarrass his former mentor.

Dr. Melrose blinked and after a split-second hesitation carried on, paying no more attention to Robin's response.

"Our third panelist for this evening's session is the delightful Ruthie Westover... uhh, Dr. Westover," he corrected himself a little too obviously and a little too patronizingly.

Dr. Melrose smiled as he said it, and Ruthie nodded in his direction.

"Dr. Westover studied at Miami University in Oxford, Ohio, and then went on to become one of the best doctoral students ever turned out by Tulane University. We at Jericho State University were lucky to land her amidst all the competition for her... um... skills and talents ... As we all expected, she has been so successful that she was offered early promotion and tenure and is now under consideration for promotion to Full Professor.

"Dr. Westover is very well-known regionally for her work in the psychology of sex. She has combined both theory *and* practice..." and he smiled what looked like a self-indulgent smirk, "...by which I mean private therapy practice, of course, ... in ways that differentiate her from other therapists. Her research relies on the Freudian foundations I have expounded, but she seems to be taking those concepts in different directions that appear to be at odds with my earlier work. I'm sure that as the discussion proceeds this evening, we will be able to iron out our difficulties..."

In her most flirtatious voice, Ruthie responded, "Yes, James, I'm sure we'll be able to work on our differences. But do they all have to be resolved in your favor before I can be promoted to full professor?"

Dr. Melrose seemed flustered. He always responded positively to Ruthie's flirty ways; he couldn't help himself, and he even felt slightly aroused right then. He was momentarily at a loss for words, but he rebounded with, "Well, Dr. Westover, you must know that the decision about your promotion is not mine alone; it's up to the entire promotion committee to determine when, not if, I assure you, but when to promote you."

Ruthie actually cooed, "Thank you, James..."

Half the people in the room were impressed. They couldn't believe she had been so blatant in her sex-laden come-hither tone of voice, and they couldn't believe it might be effective.

The other half of the room were disgusted by it. "How dare she try to use sex or even intimate that she would be willing to use sex to get what she wants!" opined Stephen Stubbins from The University of Oklahoma, but he reluctantly (and silently and wistfully) admitted to himself that it would probably work on him if she wanted anything from him. In general, the men in the room were both impressed and jealous, hoping she would show some interest in them. The women in the room were silently seething because Ruthie was so obviously using sex appeal to get what she wanted, and they all knew that she out-classed them in that competitive arena when men were the judges.

The tensions in the room mounted, as they often did when Ruthie and Dr. Melrose had an exchange. People began to stir, exhibiting mild discomfort, feeling ill-at-ease around Ruthie's cooing and dreading any confrontations that might emerge. Some shuffled their feet; others made their way to the bar to get drink refills; some murmured quietly to each other; still others looked at the floor, as if they were intensely interested in the patterns of the floor tiles.

Dr. Melrose tried to act as if he was oblivious to the mood of the room, despite the heat he was feeling himself, but he failed miserably. As the commotion grew, he looked at Phillipa, and she immediately knew what to do. He wouldn't clink on a glass himself because doing that was beneath him; instead, he relied on Phillipa to help him regain the floor.

Phillipa picked up a pen and tapped on her wine glass, getting everyone to quiet down.

Without acknowledging her, Dr. Melrose blithely carried on. "Last, and certainly not least," he smiled at his obvious and unsubtle self-praise, "There's my own presentation, which will wrap up this evening's session and tie everything together. In it, I will endeavor to show how nearly all of the recent work in the psychology of sex that isn't fatally flawed supports my original work which Dr. Westover has so kindly often referred to as 'foundational'.

"As you can tell from these brief introductions, not all of our panelists deal explicitly with the psychology of sex, but as good Freudians we all know that sex is at the heart of every issue, right?" and while Dr. Melrose laughed at his own joke, others laughed along, more out of sense of embarrassment or obligation.

Again, he looked at Phillipa. And again, she started the applause.

Chapter 10 -- **Mingling**

When the applause died down, Dr. Melrose told Phillipa to bring him a cup of de-caffeinated coffee. "Check to see if any of the other panelists would like some coffee, too. And get one for yourself, too, if you'd like." He said it all as if it was an order, but he didn't bark out orders; rather, he spoke as someone who was used to telling people what to do.

Phillipa saw it as part of her job – Dr. Melrose told her what to do, and she did it, and so she took orders for coffee from each of the other panelists, asking how they'd like their coffee. She lingered with Andy Kopfmann, trying to engage him in conversation.

"How would you like your coffee, Andy?"

"Oh, just one cream, no sugar will be fine, thanks."

"Can I get you anything else while I'm getting the coffee?"

"No, thanks. The coffee will be good, though."

She moved on to get the coffee orders from the rest of the panelists, but she didn't offer to get anything else for any of the others...

A few minutes later, Phillipa returned with a cardboard carrying tray holding five styrofoam cups. She had used a pen to write Dr.M, AK, RB, RW, or Ph on each of the cups so that each session participant would get the cup of coffee fixed up the way they wanted it. The one marked Ph was hers.

- - -

Lieutenant Randall heard about everything that had transpired from those who were attending the session. Also, it turned out that Sam Vanderstadt, a graduate student in psychology at The University of Indiana, was attending the session and had used his smartphone to video the introductions along with the responses. He was planning to record the entire session, if he could, but after the introductions, he turned his phone off to save space and to save his phone's battery.

The lieutenant apologized to Sam and said, "I'm sorry. I know this will inconvenience you for a day or two, but we'll need to take your phone with us for now. Once we download whatever videos you took this evening, we'll get the phone back to you. I'll try to have one of our tech guys get onto it first thing tomorrow morning. We won't look at anything else on the phone, and we won't keep copies of any files other than what you have shot here this evening, I assure you.

Sam insisted on a receipt and added a clause to the receipt stating everything Lieutenant Randall had promised. He hoped it would protect his privacy, but he realized that no matter what was on the receipt, the police might look at and copy more than they should. He sighed a sigh of relief that the only videos on his phone were from previous sessions of the ASP conference.

- - -

The half hour after Dr. Melrose finished the introductions dragged on to nearly forty-five minutes; and to fill the time, people mingled, sipped drinks, and chatted with each other. At one point, Robin worked his way over to Ruthie and asked, "So, Ruthie, how's it going?"

"Just fine, thanks," She almost sneered. "Same as it was when we had dinner with James, earlier this evening."

She looked away. That kind of opening from him was pathetic, and they both knew it, but Robin persisted. "You've done pretty well for yourself so far, haven't you... Tenure and a promotion early in your career, and did I hear James announce that you're in line for maybe another promotion soon? And who knows, maybe even an endowed chair in psychology eventually? That's quite impressive."

"Thanks. I've worked hard, and you know it. I deserve all that and more."

"So, tell me, Ruthie, are you still using puddings in all your research experiments and in your counselling exercises?"

"Listen, Rob Bob," Ruthie sounded exasperated. "You can read all the details about my research and counselling techniques in the articles I publish. They're all listed and available on the psychology department website."

Robin reacted with a bit of hurt and a bit of anger. He

was trying to flirt with Ruthie, and she put him down pretty coldly. It was a clear rejection.

"Ruthie, you know I hated that nickname when you used it, even when we were together."

"I like it. It suits you."

"But you know *I* don't like it. My name is Robin."

"Okay, Robbie Bobbie." Ruthie smirked.

"So... tell me, Ruthie, which flavor of pudding are you using these days? As I recall, you used to be partial to butterscotch pudding, is that right? Or has your repertoire grown to include the use of chocolate and vanilla now and then, too, just to add some variety to your research and therapy? You know what they say, 'Variety is the spice of life.' "

"Robbie, you know I believe in client-centered therapy. I let the clients choose. They're happier that way, and, more importantly, my therapy seems to have noticeably better results when *they* choose."

"Right," Robin replied, dripping with sarcasm. "You let them choose which pudding to use, but you don't let them choose whether to use any pudding at all. What kind of 'client-centered' therapy is that?" he asked using his fingers to make air quotes around 'client-centered'. "It sounds pretty controlling, if you ask me..."

"Well, Robbie Bobbie, they always have a choice. There are lots of other therapists they can choose from. They don't have to go through the therapy regime I have devised; it's their choice. They can always go to someone else... Or, if they're really desperate, they can call you on one of your counselling programs..." Ruthie matched him sarcasm for sarcasm as she made her eyes big, as if in wonderment, "... or maybe they'll even be lucky enough to appear on television with you! The world-famous Dr. Robin Bobbitt!"

She snorted a "Hmph," and added, "a doctor? You? A doctor? I laugh."

Just then Dr. Melrose approached the two of them. Robin turned to him and said quite loudly enough for others standing near them to hear, "We've just been discussing Ruthie's use of pudding in her research and counselling, Dr. Melrose. As I recall, when I was a student here, she favored butterscotch pudding, but I've been wondering whether she has moved on to chocolate or vanilla pudding at this point..."

Dr. Melrose smiled.

"Far be it from me to answer your question, *Doctor* Bobbitt," he said, emphasizing 'Doctor' just a bit too much for it to be polite.

"Well which pudding does she use when she's with you, Dr. Melrose?"

Dr. Melrose was quite taken aback. He was so flustered, he just blubbered, "What? What are you implying?..."

Robin continued, "I mean, I'm not asking about her research or counselling techniques at this point. I'm just asking about what happens with you..."

Dr. Melrose turned away in disgust. He had enjoyed some of Ruthie's experiments with vanilla pudding himself, in his office, but he was not going to let on to anyone about those times that they had spent together. He assumed that Phillipa knew, or could easily have guessed, what happened during Ruthie's extended office visits, but he was sure that she knew better than to say anything.

Just as he turned away, Andy Kopfmann approached him from where he had been waiting with his coffee next to the speakers' table.

"Say, Dr. Melrose, I was just wondering if you were able to locate any fugu to serve with the hors d'oeuvres this evening. Remember I wrote you about that last month? It's a very interesting seafood delicacy that I've had several times in Vancouver and in Asia, but it must be prepared properly..."

"I had Phillipa look into that, Dr. Kopfmann" answered Dr. Melrose dismissively. He was still shaken by Robin's intrusive questions, "But she couldn't find any place that could get fugu for us, and even if she could locate a supply of the fish, she couldn't find any chef in the area who had even the faintest idea about how to prepare it."

"Well, thanks for trying."

He wandered back to the head table to pick up his cup of coffee and then searched the room, hoping to speak with Ruthie some more.

Chapter 11 – **Unethical Behavior**

After Andy walked away, Dr. Dwayne Carter approached Dr. Melrose.

Lieutenant Randall asked him, "What was your conversation with Dr. Melrose about?"

"I'm a dream therapist," he replied, "and dream therapy, as you may know, owes its origins to Freudian analysis."

"Yes?"

"That's if you discount ancient Greece and Rome and Shakespeare," Dr. Carter smiled. "Anyway, we had a good chuckle together about one of my recent cases – a woman who dreamed she was standing in a rowboat in the middle of a lake..."

Lieutenant Randall had no idea where that was going, but he did vaguely catch on that the symbolism of the dream sounded phallic. He smiled a bit, with the corners of his mouth barely turning up, and said, "And? ..."

"We had a good laugh about it. That's all," Dr. Carter continued. "And then Dr. Melrose asked how much 'private' therapy I had to give the woman, and we laughed about that, too."

"Why laugh?"

"He was making a very strong suggestion that she had strong sexual needs that I should offer to satisfy. He had a reputation for doing that himself, though he was never accused of anything explicitly by any of his own patients. Well, there were complaints, but nothing ever came of them..."

Lieutenant Randall raised his eyebrows, as if he was asking Dr. Carter to elaborate.

Dr. Carter continued, "To be honest with you, I laughed mostly because he still is a don of the profession; actually, I was uncomfortable with his response."

"Why did you tell him about the case, then? Didn't you anticipate something like that would happen if he has that reputation?"

"Point made and taken," answered Dr. Carter. "As I said, though, he is ... or rather he was ... a don in the field. I expected he would like the story. That's all."

"Isn't it unethical," asked Lieutenant Randall, "to share confidential information about your patients?"

"Of course it is, but we do it all the time, and it isn't considered unethical if we do it anonymously. Maybe you weren't aware of this, but the counseling journals are full of case studies where therapists share stories and discussions about very interesting cases. And for this case, there was no way Dr. Melrose could identify her; she doesn't live anywhere near the Midwest."

"Okay. But you say Dr. Melrose had a reputation for sleeping with his patients?"

Dr. Carter hesitated and then murmured, "Good god, what I have gotten myself into here?"

"Well?" asked Lieutenant Randall...

"They're only rumours. I probably shouldn't have said anything. There were a couple of vague complaints to the APA about him..."

"The APA? What's that?" interrupted Lieutenant Randall.

"The American Psychological Association. Anyway, there was never any evidence that he did anything unethical. He was notified that there had been complaints, and it was strongly suggested that he avoid compromising situations with his clients to avoid even the appearance of unethical behavior, but there were no hearings, and there were no sanctions or reprimands."

Lieutenant Randall thought to himself, "Hmmm. Where there's smoke..."

He continued, following up his question, "What do you think, Dr. Carter? Just roughly speaking, do you think he had sex with some of his patients?"

Again Dr. Carter hesitated. "Even though he's dead, I want to be careful how I word this. Let me say ... 'I wouldn't be surprised to learn he did.' Does that give you enough of an answer?"

"For now that will do. Thank you."

- - -

Lieutenant Randall called his sergeants over. "Scheffler, Houston, go back over everything with each of the people in this room, and do it privately. Find out if any of them had ever been patients of Dr. Melrose. If so, we'll want to spend some time talking with them in greater detail."

Then he called Phillipa back to ask her a few more questions.

"Ms. MaGraw, first of all, do you know who we should call or notify about Dr. Melrose? Did he have a wife or family or someone we should notify?"

"Not really," Phillipa answered. "We used to joke together that if anything happened to one of us, people should probably notify the other person, but we never wrote that down or did anything about it. I think he has some relatives somewhere out in California. He goes out there to visit once every few years, but he's never said much about them. You'll have to check his files to see about that."

"Okay, thanks." And then Lieutenant Randall changed topics. "Do you know if any of the people in this room were ever patients of Dr. Melrose?"

"I can see at least two people here who were his patients at one time or another. None recently, though. Why?"

Lieutenant Randall tried to be careful and was purposely vague.

"Do you think any of them might have had a grudge against Dr. Melrose?"

"Maybe. Not all of his patients were grateful for the insights that Dr. Melrose provided. But I never thought any of them were bothered enough to want him dead...."

"Do me a favor, then, and sit over here." He tore a sheet out of his notebook. "Please write down the names of these two and any others here who might have seen him professionally, in his capacity as a therapist. Look around the room carefully and don't leave anyone out. When you're finished, I'd like you to stand here with me and tell me who each of the people are."

"I can't do that. They'll know I told you."

"Patient files may be confidential, but patient lists are not. You must know that. We can get a court order for a list of all of Dr. Melrose's patients, but it will be much better if we question these folks while they're here, right now. We'll re-question everyone to some extent, so don't worry, we'll just work our way into it. They won't suspect anything."

"Well, okay, but if you're going to interrogate everyone again, you just need the list, you don't need me to point them out, do you?"

"Fair enough. As long as we have your list, we'll be able to double check their answers to see if any of them deny having been patients when actually they were."

And he called the sergeants and other investigators back. "There's only one good way to do this, I think. Each of you follow up on someone you didn't question initially. Begin by asking what they saw, and we'll compare and compile their answers later. Then ask if they or any of their relatives or friends were ever patients of Dr. Melrose and get the names of anyone who was. Push pretty far with this. Find out if they were happy with his therapy. And find out if they felt pushed or maybe even bullied by him, even slightly. And ask them if they had sex with him or if he ever suggested it or tried to come on to them, and watch their reactions."

Sergeant Scheffler looked wary and confused. "Both sexes?" he asked.

Lieutenant Randall hadn't considered the possibilities, but quickly said, "Absolutely. Who knows what he was into. The hints we're getting so far suggest anything might have been possible with him."

Meanwhile, the Butts and Holly teams had left the room with Dr. Melrose. Lieutenant Randall could hear the shouting from the members of the media in the hallway as the investigative teams ran the gauntlet to get back to their offices and start work.

⚥

Chapter 12 – After the Introductions

When Dr. Melrose finished speaking with Dr. Carter, he found his way back to the head table, where Phillipa was talking with Andy Kopfmann.

As they stood there together sipping their coffee, he asked, "Phillipa, what is taking so long for those people to find and bring the equipment? How long can it take to unplug a projector and move it?"

"I really don't know, Dr. Melrose, but it's a bit more involved than just unplugging and moving a slide projector. It's the whole computer-projector system that needs to be shut down and moved. Would you like me to go check on them?"

"That would be helpful."

As she was turning to leave, Dr. Melrose stopped her, reaching out and touching her left elbow. Phillipa knew what that meant. He only touched her elbow like that when he was about to suggest they go to bed together.

"I wonder what happened..." thought Phillipa. "Did he already try it with Ruthie and get rejected? And what about the other women in this room? That Shari McBride sitting over by the door by herself keeps looking at him as if she'd be interested. Why me?"

She kept these thoughts to herself, though.

Instead, she smiled at Dr. Melrose and said, "Yes?" but it wasn't quite a question and wasn't quite an answer to his unstated invitation.

She knew what he wanted, and he knew that she knew. And to uncomplicate things, she knew that he knew that she knew... but they left everything unsaid. Phillipa smiled again and nodded. They didn't need to exchange any words about it. They just knew. She no longer worshipped the man; in fact, in some ways she didn't like him or respect him. Nevertheless, they had a history, and their relationship suited her in many ways.

Phillipa had hoped to spend some time with Andy Kopfmann later that evening, but as usual he gave no indication of being interested in her. In her mind going to bed with Dr. Melrose would be better than pining for Andy Kopfmann.

What Phillipa hoped didn't show on her face, though, was that she wasn't giving up on Andy. She thought that if she could spend any time with Andy at all, she wanted to do that, even if it wasn't romantic time. Her hope was that if she could spend some time with him, well...who knew what might develop from that.

Also, she knew that Dr. Melrose could easily abandon her if he was able to interest Ruthie or maybe someone else in the room. She resented his taking her for granted and abandoning her whenever any other options came along. And yet she didn't want to say 'no' to him; there were still things she liked or even loved about the man and, more importantly, she loved her job and didn't want to jeopardize it.

Within five minutes, Phillipa was back in the room.

"Dr. Melrose, those idiots from the hotel were waiting in the hallway until one of the speakers finished before they would disrupt that session. I lit a fire under their behinds by opening the door to that session and then yelling at them to go in and retrieve the equipment right then. The folks in that room were not altogether pleased with the interruption, but they stopped their presentations while the hotel I-T people went in to get the computer projector setup. I expect them to be here soon, and we should be ready to roll in no more than ten or fifteen minutes."

"Thanksh, Phillipa," and they raised their coffee cups as he saluted her with a silent toast, and she accepted it.

"Thanksh?" Phillipa wondered. It was a barely perceptible slurring of his words, as she recalled it later, and it puzzled her because she didn't think Dr. Melrose had had any alcohol to drink that evening.

- - -

Dr. Carter had never met Ruthie Westover, but her reputation preceded her, and so he wasn't surprised when she approached him that evening. He was on the faculty at Yale University, and she was known to be ambitious. Yale had actually considered offering her a job when she left graduate school at Tulane, but the general sense among those on the hiring committee had been that her research would never be top-flight. Dr. Holland, who was chair of Yale's psychology department at the time, told his fellow faculty members that she would be a very interesting but also very disruptive colleague. From what Dr. Carter had observed so far that evening, he could see what Dr. Holland meant.

"Dr. Carter?" cooed Ruthie. "May I introduce myself? I'm Dr. Westover, but you probably know that already since we panelists were all introduced just a few moments ago..."

She put out her hand for Dr. Carter to shake. Her grasp was both firm and warm. As she did that, she also sized him up: "Hmmm," she thought to herself. "Late forties, trim; high forehead and slightly receding hairline; blonde hair; contacts. A perfect man to get to know better tonight, now and later..."

Dr. Carter later admitted to himself that he felt a sense of excitement when they shook hands. He wasn't sure whether the excitement was because of her reputation, her cooing, or her body language when they shook hands, but he felt the sexual energy emanating from Ruthie.

"I'm pleased to meet you, Dr. Westover."

Dr. Carter wasn't sure what she wanted, but he was too polite to bluntly ask her.

He didn't have to wait long for her to tell him.

"Dr. Carter, are you at all familiar with my research and my therapy techniques?"

During her earlier repartee with Dr. Bobbitt, he had heard considerable inuendo about her use of puddings and he was curious.

"No, I'm afraid all I know is what I overheard earlier this evening. I gather you make extensive use of puddings?

He felt another tingle with sexual overtones.

"Well, yes, I do, and that has become a problem for my   career..."

"How is that?"

"Even though I have had considerable success with my therapeutic techniques using puddings, they are seen by some people in the profession as gimmicky or too *avant garde*. The result is that my research isn't viewed as being sufficiently solid or scientific to merit the promotion that Dr. Melrose mentioned earlier..."

She blinked her eyes at him. Blinked once, not batted. The single blink had a deliberateness to it that Dr. Carter had rarely seen before. Ruthie developed the technique while she was in graduate school because batting her eyes was too obvious, attracted the wrong type of attention too often, and was frequently off-putting; but a single blink still created the aura of sex appeal that she made effective use of, in combination with her petite frame and tight skirt.

Dr. Carter wasn't necessarily taken in by the sex appeal of her eye blink, but he was intrigued, even flattered, by Ruthie's overall flirtiness.

"Well," he said, "is there some way for you to beef up the research side of your work? Some way to maybe do comparisons with random trials or something like that?"

"Oh, what a brilliant idea!" Ruthie controlled herself just enough to sound enthusiastic without gushing. "I think I've been so convinced that my therapeutic techniques are right that I can't bear the thought of not using them with all my clients. How would you recommend that I go about doing what you suggest?"

She was still cooing, but in moderation.

"Why not partner with someone who doesn't use your techniques?" suggested Dr. Carter. "It would take some work to make sure you control for a lot of other variables, but I see no reason why comparison trials would have to be carried out with the same therapist, especially in your case. You would probably have trouble using any technique that isn't your own, right?"

"Oh, you are so right!" and then she got to one of the topics she hoped to raise with Dr. Carter. "Do you have any colleagues at Yale who might be interested in this type of project?"

"Ideally, I should think it would be better if you could partner with someone here in Illinois – maybe at Chicago or at Champaign-Urbana? Or maybe Washington University in St. Louis or the University of Wisconsin up in Madison? That way you could possibly sit in on each other's sessions or at least be close enough to collaborate in person. Let me think about it."

Dr. Carter wasn't about to offer the names of any of his colleagues without discussing it with them first, but he didn't want to put her off, either.

"Why don't you send me copies of your papers," he said. "I'll look at them and see if I can recommend anyone..."

Even though Ruthie had just snubbed Robin by telling him that her research papers were listed on the Jericho State Psychology Department website, she wanted to be accommodating with Dr. Carter. She really wanted him and others at Yale to read her papers so that they could understand her techniques more fully.

"That would be terrific, Dr. Carter. Meanwhile, why don't we go for a drink together after this session, and I can explain my techniques in more detail..."

He was clearly flustered; he even blushed a bit. He knew he had blushed and that Ruthie had seen it.

She had had the desired effect, she thought; but he resisted.

"That would be good," he said, "but not for too long. I'm really sorry ... I mean it ... but I need to get through reading and grading some student papers I've brought along, and as things stand with the delays here, I'll need to burn the midnight oil for that job."

He'd have enjoyed spending time with Ruthie with the expectation that eventually she would demonstrate some of her techniques for him in his hotel room. He was disappointed and he showed it.

Ruthie was disappointed, too, and she showed it, too. She had hoped, if nothing else, to get Dr. Carter onside for her appeal to the promotion committee at Jericho State.

She rebounded quickly.

"I'd offer to help with your grading, but I don't think that would work very well," she smiled seductively, "but I'll be sure to email you copies of some of my better papers. And I'll look forward to getting your feedback."

Their entire exchange had been academic and completely proper, but they both recognized all the none-too-subtle sexual undertones.

"Two ships passing in the night," thought Dr. Carter as he left Ruthie and made his way to the bar. "And maybe that's just as well..."

Meanwhile Ruthie went back to the head table to pick up her coffee and survey the room.

Sam Vanderstadt, the graduate student from Indiana, later told the investigators that she looked like a hawk, searching for new prey. "She kept scanning the room, as if she was looking for someone to approach about something. She was a bit old for me, but I'd have been game if she had let her gaze rest on me for even a moment."

Chapter 13 – Looking for Details

Lieutenant Mike Randall didn't have a commanding presence. He was 5'10" and weighed about 180 lbs. He was clean-shaven with thinning dark brown hair, and he wore inexpensive dark suits with well-polished black shoes when he was on the job.

He was 46 years old, married, and had three children. As a career police officer, he had slowly worked his way up through the ranks with solid, competent police work. He was neither the blustering buffoon of some mystery novels nor the brilliant rebel of others. He was an ordinary yet above average cop with above average skills and a strong sense of integrity.

As he stood at the doorway to the room, he wondered about the people there, all of them interested in the psychology of sex, and most of them working or counseling or doing who-knows-what in that area. His own attitude was that he didn't want to look into it too much. He and his wife had an okay marriage and a good life. The only problem in their marriage was that he was gone from home long hours during the early stages of an investigation, but they had done their best to work out different ways to deal with the demands of his job.

When he got the call to look into a possibly suspicious death at the Jericho Hilton, he phoned his wife, Louise, to let her know he'd be home late. "Lou, the officers on the scene say there are fifty or so suspects," he told her. "It'll be until the wee hours of the morning before we let them go, and unless it turns out to be death from natural causes, we'll be at it again early tomorrow morning."

Five years ago, Lieutenant Randall was moved from robbery into the homicide division, and he enjoyed it, aside from the hours. There had been only one case in those five years that he hadn't been able to solve, but he had been successful in both investigating and seeing convictions in all the other cases assigned to him. To his dismay, the convictions were rarely for first-degree murder, though, because, as the District Attorney argued, it was cheaper and more efficient to "plead 'em down" to get the cases closed.

- - -

During the first hour after Dr. Melrose stumbled into the room, the place was especially crowded. Not only were all fifty session attendees being kept there, but the medical examiner's team with Dr. Butts, the forensics team headed up by Bob Holly, and all the extra investigators that Lieutenant Randall had asked for were there, too.

On top of all that, the I-T people from the hotel had shown up with the computer, projector, and connecting cords, ready to set up all the equipment. Without knowing everything Phillipa had done to yell at them and pressure them into getting the equipment there quickly, Lieutenant Randall didn't understand why they seemed so upset when he shooed them away unceremoniously.

The notice on the back of the door said that according to the Fire Marshall the room could hold 120 people safely, but it felt congested with everyone who was there while Lieutenant Randall and the investigators tried to corral them and then separate and isolate them for questioning.

- - -

As the other investigators began questioning everyone else in the room, Sergeants Houston and Scheffler focused on those who had left the room while Dr. Melrose was out. They began by tag-teaming Phillipa.

Sergeant Houston started, "Ms. MaGraw, why did you leave the room shortly after Dr. Melrose did?"

"Andy Kopfmann wanted me to set up an appointment for him to meet with Dr. Melrose tomorrow. I suggested we should wait until after the session to make the appointment because I didn't have Dr. Melrose's appointment book with me, but he said he wasn't sure he'd be available later. I think he was hoping to invite Ruthie Westover out for a drink or something. So anyway, since the session wasn't going to start for at least another fifteen minutes yet, I decided to go out to the parking lot to get Dr. Melrose's appointment book. It was in my shoulder bag, which was locked in the trunk of my car."

"Why didn't you have your shoulder bag with you here in the room for the session?" asked Sergeant Houston. Sergeant Ellie Houston had been on the force for eight years and had worked on the homicide team with Lieutenant Randall and Sergeant Scheffler for the past four years. Some of her co-officers thought she was a bit too soft, but Sergeant Scheffler and Lieutenant Randall knew otherwise. She had a caring streak to her, but she wasn't afraid of controversy or hard work or even physically challenging situations. At five-eight and 175 pounds, she could hold her own with most criminals, in part because she was a tough nut inside her soft, sensitive shell.

She continued, "Weren't there things in your shoulder bag that you might want if Dr. Melrose asked for them?"

"Maybe, but not ordinarily. Besides, look at my bag."

Phillipa gestured.

"It's that monstrous thing on that chair over there. Everyone always teases me that it's really a big briefcase with a shoulder strap, and I suppose it is in some ways. Last year at Christmas the grad students in the psych department gave me a luggage carrier with wheels as a sort of gag gift. I've tried it a few times, but it's too cumbersome to use regularly. I do carry this small clutch bag with my essentials in it, though."

Sergeant Scheffler stepped in, "You didn't think you would need his appointment book here, where others might want to make appointments to see him while they're here at the conference?"

Sergeant Jason Scheffler had been on the homicide team longer than Sergeant Houston, but he usually let her take the lead. His questions tended to be more of the follow-up nature. He wasn't known for his creativity or his brilliance; put simply, he was an adequate cop.

"I probably should have anticipated that I might need my bag," Phillipa sighed. "But I didn't want to be encumbered by that huge thing, so I took a chance and left the appointment book in the bag in my trunk. That was a mistake, I see now, in retrospect, but at the time it seemed like an okay decision."

That all fit with what others said: Phillipa had her shoulder bag with her when she re-entered the room just after Dr. Melrose had collapsed on the floor.

"According to several people, you came back into the room only seconds after Dr. Melrose stumbled in. Did you see him outside?"

"No, I didn't. I stopped in the ladies' room to freshen up after I got back from my car, and I must have just missed him."

Sergeant Scheffler made a note in his book to see if there was some way to check on that, possibly using the hotel's security video system.

"So tell us what happened. Why was Dr. Kopfmann so insistent on setting up an appointment tomorrow with Dr. Melrose?"

"He said he wanted to talk with him about how he was referring to his work..."

Sergeant Scheffler interrupted her, "He? Him? His? Can you run that past us again with names?"

Exasperated, but mostly embarrassed, Phillipa sighed again and then repeated slowly, "Andy said he wanted to talk with Dr. Melrose about how Dr. Melrose was referring to Andy's work."

"I see. Thanks. But why was he so insistent about setting up the appointment tonight?"

Phillipa replied, "There were a couple of reasons. First, Andy is leaving the day after tomorrow to fly back to Liechtenstein, where he's working now, and he wanted to make sure they could meet tomorrow. And second, I think he was pretty bothered by the way Dr. Melrose had represented his work and he wanted to make sure there was enough time for them to have a lengthy discussion about it."

Sergeant Houston resumed the questioning. "Did you have to go to your car to get Dr. Melrose's appointment book right then? Couldn't it have waited until after the session was over?"

"That's what I suggested, but as I told you already, Andy seemed to think he might be busy then..."

- - -

When they quizzed Andy about it, he agreed with the substance of what Phillipa said.

"Yes, I did want to meet with Dr. Melrose tomorrow. After hearing the argument about how he had stiffed Robin out of thousands of dollars of referral fees, I wanted to make sure he was still going to cover my transportation expenses to come to this conference. And I needed to get some things straight with him about how he was misrepresenting my research. He

97

kept saying my results corroborated his early, so-called seminal research, but they didn't. Not really. I knew we wouldn't have time to get down to the nitty gritty of the differences during the discussion period tonight, and I wanted to talk about it further with him tomorrow."

"In the end," Andy added, "It turns out I didn't have to worry about the travel expenses. Phillipa looks after all those things, and she has assured me I'll be fully compensated for them."

Sergeant Scheffler spoke calmly and softly, "Tell us what happened, exactly."

"Well, I tried to speak with Dr. Melrose tonight, but he seemed reluctant to get into a prolonged discussion here before the session began. I can understand why, in front of all these people he's been trying to impress for decades. Anyway, he told me to speak to Phillipa to make an appointment.

"When I did that, she said she didn't have his appointment book up here with her – it was in her car – and she suggested she take me out for a drink afterward and we could set up the appointment then. I told her I probably had other plans and so she said something like, 'Okay, why don't I go get it now? It looks as if we'll still have a bit of a wait for the hotel staff to bring the projector and set it up.'"

"*Did* you have other plans?"

Andy was caught off guard by the question.

"Not really, but I hoped to... I wanted to keep my options open..." and he held back a big grin, turning it into just a hint of a smile.

Sergeant Houston, in true tag-team fashion, pushed a bit. "What does that mean exactly?"

Andy sighed an embarrassed sigh. "Okay, back when I was a graduate student and Ruthie was a young hotshot professor, she and I had brief thing together. I was hoping to rekindle something with her while I'm here."

"What happened?"

"Back then? We had a fling, and I quite enjoyed it, the brief time we were together. I wanted to renew it while we were both here at the conference, but she wasn't very encouraging."

"No, I mean what happened to your plans to rekindle something with her tonight?"

"Do we have to go into this? Guys don't really like talking about their failures much, you know."

"It's a murder investigation."

"Well, okay. I tried to chat her up, but she was barely polite and certainly not encouraging. I think she was working on plans to advance her career in other ways..."

Back to Sergeant Scheffler. "What does that mean?"

"She spent a lot of time talking quietly with Dr. Carter. He's from Yale and could be a valuable contact for many of us here. I think she was hoping to influence him and get his help for advancing her career at Jericho State ... or maybe she was even hoping to entice him into suggesting that she apply for a position at Yale."

He went on, "I don't think it was working though. I saw Dr. Carter walk away from her, looking almost relieved, and after that she stood up at the head table for a while peering over the rim of her cup of coffee, looking around as if she was trying to decide who might be the next best person to approach. When I saw that, I thought maybe I'd have a chance to get lucky tonight after all..."

"The way several people have described things, it sounds as if Phillipa MaGraw might have had some interest in you..."

"Oh, ... Well, I suppose. Maybe so. But it wasn't going to happen. She's really nice and all that, but I wasn't interested."

"Why not?"

Andy frowned. "I know this is a murder investigation, but do you really need to go into this?"

He sighed but continued. "Anyway, the truth is that when I first met her, she looked just like a neighbor we had when I was growing up in Nanaimo, a woman who terrorized our family. I couldn't get past that resemblance back when I was a grad student. I tried to overlook the resemblance because, after all, Phillipa is a really decent woman, but I just couldn't do it. She doesn't resemble that woman so much anymore though... hmmm... well, anyway, I hadn't ever thought about her as anything other than a friend.

Sergeant Houston stepped back in and said, "One more thing we need to ask you, Dr. Kopfmann."

"Sure."

"Why did you leave the room when Dr. Melrose did?"

"I didn't leave **when** he did. It must have been a few minutes or so after he left. I just went to check on him, to make sure he was okay."

"Was there any reason for you to think he wasn't okay?"

"He had been gone quite a while and I knew he would want the session to get going again as soon as the projection equipment arrived. Well, that, and he did loosen his necktie as he was leaving the room. That seemed odd for him, given that he saw this session as a special occasion that was sort of in his honor."

Chapter 14 – Getting the Timeline Straight

Together, the sergeants interviewed Ruthie next.

Sergeant Houston began, "After Dr. Melrose introduced all of you, what happened then?"

"We all just milled around, talking with each other."

"Let me be more specific, then. What did *you* do next? What part of the room did you go to and who did you speak with?"

Ruthie frowned. "I think the first thing I did after the introductions was move quickly to get away from Andy."

"What was that about? Why?"

Ruthie knew she had opened herself up for this by telling them what she had done, but Andy had been a pest and she wouldn't mind some help in keeping him at bay.

"Andy and I had a very, *very* brief affair many, many years ago. He wouldn't let it go back then, and the way he was following me around tonight, it looked as if he was still carrying a torch. He didn't know how to take 'no' for an answer then, and I was afraid he still didn't. I certainly didn't want him hovering around me."

"When you got away from him, where did you go? Who did you speak with?"

"I saw some people gathered around Dr. Carter -- he's a big-name dream specialist from Yale – and I joined them. After a few minutes of meaningless chitchat with them, he turned his attention to me, and I introduced myself."

She smiled, indicating that she believed she had won some sort of prize by attracting Dr. Carter's attention away from all the others who were talking with him.

"What did you talk about?" Sergeant Houston continued.

"I had hoped to be able spend some time with him to explain my research to him. At the very least I wanted his help as a reference in my plan to be promoted at Jericho State; but in the longer-run, I was looking for an in at Yale. I thought he might be able to help me along those lines."

"How long did you talk with him?" asked Sergeant Scheffler.

"Oh ... I don't know. I have no idea."

"Just a rough idea then?"

"Maybe five minutes, but not more than ten minutes for sure."

"Okay," said Sergeant Houston. "How did he respond?"

"I think he was pretty favourably inclined, but we didn't have nearly enough time to talk here, before the   session."

"Did you agree to meet later then?"

"No!"

Ruthie wasn't about to admit to the police that she had hoped to seduce Dr. Carter and had gotten a brush-off.

Sergeant Houston then asked, "What happened next?"

"Dr. Carter excused himself and headed for the bar. I didn't want to seem pushy, so I went back to the head table and picked up my coffee and stood there, sipping it, looking around at the room."

"And then?"

"That goofy looking guy over there with the bright plaid sportcoat and bow tie ... what's his name? ... something like Robert or Rodney or something? ... I know, it's Roddie. Roddie Castman. I think he teaches somewhere up in Wisconsin, maybe at one of their lesser state schools. Anyway, he came over to hit on me."

"What happened?"

"Oh, the usual with men like him. It's a standard, boring, easily predicted script: They find out a woman does unusual work in sex therapy and the psychology of sex, and they start drooling. They just automatically assume I'll sleep with them. It's disgusting. He started the way they always do, 'So, tell me, Dr. Westover, how do you use puddings in your sex therapy'?"

Sergeant Scheffler couldn't control his curiosity, and Ruthie knew she had him hooked. He showed that he was a bit more subtle than most men, though, by asking, "What did you tell him?"

"The same thing I tell everyone else who is too lazy to read my papers: 'I have my clients sit across a table from each other and look at each other for two minutes without speaking and without looking away, and then I have them slowly feed the pudding to each other.'"

"That's it?"

"Well, that's what I *told* him...." and she smiled coyly. "He can read my published articles if he seriously wants to know more about what I really do. But he doesn't. Most of them don't. He was just asking that as a transparent come on."

"What did you talk about after that?"

"It was just the usual continuation of the scripted conversation. The minute I saw him coming toward me I knew what was going to happen. He leered at me, all the time trying to look sexy and professional but just being disgusting to the point of being creepy, then he asked me about puddings and sex, and then he didn't know what else to say other than, 'Oh, that sounds very interesting. Maybe we could go out for a late snack after the session and you could tell me more?' and this jerk tonight even suggested we could find some place that serves pudding."

Ruthie seemed both disgusted and yet proud of scoring another victim. "I told him I had other plans and turned away from him."

"What happened after that?" asked Sergeant Houston.

"Robin Bobbitt headed my way. He and I had had a longish thing together back when he was in grad school, and we both knew what he wanted when he came over to speak with me." She paused and looked at both the sergeants and added very meaningfully, "You see, I'm *very* good at what I do."

"Yes, go on..." said Sergeant Scheffler in a flat voice that he hoped would reveal nothing about his interest in whatever she did or could do that she was so good at doing.

"Geez, you sound like a friggn psychiatrist or something, 'Yes, go on'? Are you for real?"

Sergeant Scheffler just kept looking at Ruthie.

After an uncomfortable pause, she continued, "Well, he and I chatted a bit. I congratulated him on his media success, and he congratulated me on my academic success. Polite back-and-forth stuff. Then I saw Andy walking toward us, and I wasn't about to make it a threesome with them ... not in *any* sense of the word. I told them, 'I have to use the ladies' room. I hope you'll excuse me.' And I left the room."

Sergeant Houston took over again.

"I know this may seem intrusive, but it looks as though something might have happened to Dr. Melrose while he was out of the room, and so I have to ask you if you encountered him while you were out..."

Ruthie sighed. "No, I didn't. But since you'll probably find this out anyway if you continue with all the questioning, I didn't use the facilities either. It looked as if either Robin or Andy might follow me and wait for me outside the restroom, and so I dodged through the kitchen area, making sure I could avoid both Robin and Andy, and I found my way out into the alley in back of the hotel. There's this really cute sous chef who was taking a break back there, too, and we shared a to... a smoke."

"Did you see Dr. Melrose at all while you were out of the room?" asked Sergeant Scheffler.

"No, of course not! I was in the back alley, and I gather he was in the men's room. And just to be clear, no, I wasn't looking for him either!"

"What about Phillipa? Did you see or encounter her while you were out? She left the room about the same time you did and says she went to her car to get Dr. Melrose's appointment book. Can you corroborate that? Did you see her while you were out?"

"No, why would I? As I said, I was in the back alley. I didn't see anyone else from the conference. Honestly, I was trying to avoid all these people. The wrong ones were interested in me, and I couldn't get enough time with the right ones. It was a mess for me, so I just needed to get out, get my head back together, and come back in ready to do battle during our presentations."

"Ready to do battle?" asked Sergeant Houston.

"You bet. I was going to make a bit of a name for myself tonight. I was hoping to do it in a nice way that wouldn't completely destroy James, but I also wanted people to recognize that my own research and therapy went well beyond his basic work from two centuries ago, or whenever it was he did it. I wanted them to see that my work was fresh, original, and even path-breaking."

Ruthie glared at them with a challenging expression as she went on, "Tell me, have you ever heard of any other counsellor or therapist who makes such creative use of puddings in their work? ... Well? Have you?"

"No, but how does that relate to doing battle?"

"It was pretty clear to everyone that James is ... was ... over the hill – in more ways than one... Oh, he had some good ideas and did some good work waaayyyy back when he was young and in his prime, but he needs Viagra just to get an idea up these days. He hasn't learned or done anything new for several decades. He keeps trying to make it sound as if everything the rest of us do is nothing more than a minor extension of his work, but that's wrong, and I was ready to do battle with him tonight."

108

"Wouldn't that hurt your chances for a promotion?" asked Sergeant Scheffler.

"Maybe, but I know I could have brought him around on that eventually," and she smiled a coy smile that implied she would use sex, if necessary, to get Dr. Melrose to support her case for promotion.

♂♀

Chapter 15 – **More Questions**

When the investigators questioned Robin about his actions that evening, he basically confirmed everything the others had said.

"Yes, I was quite upset with James. I sent dozens of patients his way and he never sent me any of the agreed upon referral fees. By my rough calculations he owed me at least four or five thousand dollars."

"Are referral fees legal or ethical in your profession?" asked Lieutenant Randall. "I don't know what is or isn't acceptable."

"Referral fees are common in the mental health fields," answered Robin. "If a doctor gets a patient who needs some counselling or therapy, they refer the patient to someone who is qualified to help. That person, in turn, pays the doctor a referral fee. Without referrals, many therapists would have trouble drumming up much business on their own."

"Are referral fees really all that ethical?"

"Of course! And if we didn't legitimize them, therapists and counsellors would all be offering bribes or substantial thank-you gifts to get referrals. Calling them referral fees keeps it all above board."

"But in your case..."

Lieutenant Randall didn't have to complete the question.

"Yes, in my case it might have looked somewhat questionable to some of my viewers and listeners. Here I am on TV or radio, trying to help people for free – well, the sponsors pay for my time on the air – but when the callers need or want more time, I just can't give it to them. I can't take on private patients and still help all the callers and visitors I work with on my programs. I need to refer them to someone else.

"And let me tell you, therapists are lined up to get referrals from me; I must have over five hundred business cards from therapists all over the country, wanting me to send business their way."

"So why might it have looked questionable?" asked Lieutenant Randall.

"The premise of my shows is that I'm a helping guy, not a money-grubbing bloodsucker. And yet that's exactly how some unsatisfied callers might see me if the idea of referral fees ever got into their heads. So I try to keep that aspect of my media work quiet."

"Why were you referring so many patients to Dr. Melrose?"

"Let's get a few things straight," answered Robin. "First of all, I wasn't sending all that many to him. I probably made upwards of four hundred referrals in the upper Midwest since he and I worked out our agreement. He got about fifty of them."

"Secondly," Robin continued, "I felt as if I owed James something. He actively supported my admission to Jericho State, and he kept me in graduate school even though several of the other professors thought I should have been booted out after my first year. He made sure I got my master's degree. Also, it has gradually become pretty clear to me that on my shows I actually use much of what I learned from him."

"But," he went on, "if some journalist wanted to cast things in a negative light, they could make it look as if I was taking bribes even though it's standard practice to make referrals and get referral fees. It might not be good for the overall image of the programs and it might affect the ratings.

"If I had collected from him, I'd have used the money to support the extension of my helping network; I wouldn't have used it personally. I shouldn't have said anything in public, as I did tonight, but James was really being quite recalcitrant about the whole thing, and it had been his idea in the first place..."

"What were you planning to do about it beyond tonight?"

"Several things. First, let me make it clear that a few thousand dollars was not really the issue; I earn a decent living with my media work and, as I said, I wasn't going to use the money personally. My problem was that I felt betrayed by James. I had already begun to refer patients to other therapists instead of him.

"But I wanted some revenge, too. I know that doesn't sound very healthy, mentally, to want revenge, but we all have feelings like that. My revenge was going to be to notify everyone who might refer patients to him about what had happened, and my confronting him publicly tonight was part of that plan. I wanted everyone in this room to know that he couldn't be trusted. He'd start out being your friend, but then he'd turn on you. I'm sure I'm not the only one who felt that way, either."

"About the time he left the room, you had a conversation with Dr. Kopfmann? What was that about?"

Robin relaxed a bit. "He and I had both dated Ruthie when we were in grad school here, and it looked as if both of us were hoping to score again tonight after the session."

Lieutenant Randall couldn't believe someone with Dr. Bobbitt's stature had really used the phrase, "score again," but he persisted.

"And?"

"We jockeyed for position. We both told lies about how *we* had broken up with *her* back then and how she wanted to get back with us. At least they were lies when I told them; and I can't imagine they weren't lies when Andy told them, too. I guess it's pretty sick, but then Ruthie has a way about her that brings those things out in men. Haven't you felt them? I mean she must have come on to you, too. After all, that's all she knows how to do socially, as far as I can tell."

Lieutenant Randall ignored the question.

"You left the room shortly after Dr. Melrose did..."

"Yes, but I think you should know, too, that toward the end of the introductions and during his conversations after them, something seemed different about James, as if he wasn't well. He spoke a bit more slowly and deliberately, and even stumbled on a few words. It wasn't extremely obvious, and most people here may not have noticed, but something seemed just a tiny bit off."

"Off? How's that?"

"Yes, off. Just before he left the room, he loosened his tie and unbuttoned the top button of his shirt. Also about then, he told Phillipa, 'I think I need to use the men's room. I'll be right back.' He wouldn't ordinarily make that sort of announcement. Freudian as he was, he was also private about his bathroom use; he normally would have just said, 'Excuse me for a moment,' and left."

"Why did you leave right after he did?"

"I don't think it was right after he left. It was another minute or two before I left. Anyway, I got a call from my producer wanting to clear up some details before tomorrow's recording session – we always record the shows two days before airing them just in case something goes wrong. I wouldn't have taken the call if the session had been running on time, as scheduled, but because of the delays in getting started, I figured 'What the heck? Why not?'"

"Okay, but why did you leave the room?"

Robin opened his hands and then gestured to the room. "Look around you and give a listen. You can hear the hubbub here now, but imagine the noise level when people are drinking and not in shock. I could barely hear anything on my phone. I had to go out into the hallway to take the call."

"So you were just out here..." Lieutenant Randall pointed to the hall right outside the door, "when Dr. Melrose returned from the men's room? You saw him stagger into the room from out here?"

"Oh, no! If I had seen that, I'd have come right in with him. No, when I talk on the phone, especially about my shows, I have to pace. I needed a quiet, less-crowded place to talk and so I found a part of the hotel where I could walk and talk in peace. I was nowhere near this room until my call was over, and then I came back here."

"Did you see anyone else from this room while you were out in hallway?"

He thought for a moment. "No, no one."

"There were four of you that we know of who left the room after Dr. Melrose left: you, Ms. MaGraw, Dr. Westover, and Dr. Kopfmann. You didn't see any of the others when you were out?"

Robin was puzzled; he had already answered that question. "I told you, no, I didn't see anyone from this room that I know while I was out in the hallways. And to be frank, I don't remember seeing *any*one that I knew out there."

"When you returned to the room, what did you see and what did you say?"

"James was lying on the floor and Phillipa was kneeling next to him. I was so angry with him I said the first vengeful thing that came to my mind, something like, 'Oh, come on, James, get up... or are you drunk *again*?'"

"What did that mean, 'drunk again'?"

"I have absolutely no idea. I don't know if he has... or should I say 'had' ... a drinking problem. I just wanted everyone in the room to think he did. He had offered me $300 when he owed me thousands, and I was determined to pay him back somehow."

"Okay, thank you. Would you mind staying here in this room for now? Thank you." Lieutenant Randall said the second 'Thank you' without waiting for a reply from Robin.

Chapter 16 – "As I Told You"

In the next round of questioning, Lieutenant Randall interviewed Andy Kopfmann.

"Tell me again why you left the room."

"As I said, I wanted to make sure Dr. Melrose was okay."

"Was there anything that made you think he might not be?"

"Hmmm. Now that you mention it... .... Hmmm.... Well, not really. I know Robin wondered if he was drunk, but I'm pretty sure he wasn't. He never drinks much, and he certainly didn't have any alcohol at dinner or while he was here in this room. I think he wanted everyone else to drink a bit to lighten up the atmosphere, but I'm pretty sure he wasn't drunk.

"Beyond that, I didn't notice anything in particular that stood out. Maybe he was speaking a little slower before he left. And maybe his steps weren't as even as they used to be, but I just chalked that up to old age. When he was leaving, he said something to Phillipa about needing to leave, but I didn't catch it."

"When you went to look for him, why didn't you go to the men's room and see him there? How could you have missed him?"

Andy was trapped.

"Okay, okay. The truth is I went out to look for Ruthie. I was hoping to speak with her and maybe suggest we get together after the session. I wandered all over the hotel, looking for her, but I couldn't find her anywhere."

"But you did see blood on the front edge of the washbasin in the men's room?"

"Yes."

"How did that happen? What I mean is, how did you happen to see it if the only reason you left the room was to look for Dr. Westover?"

"Well, when I gave up looking for Ruthie, I remembered I had told some people I was going out to look for Dr. Melrose, and so mostly to keep up appearances, I stopped in at the men's room on my way back here. I guess Dr. Melrose must have already left, but that's when I saw the blood on the front edge of the sink."

"Did you connect the blood with Dr. Melrose when you first saw it?"

"Not really. I looked at the blood and, to be honest, I thought some slob had cut himself shaving or had cut his hand or something and washed up there but didn't do a very good job of cleaning up after himself. It didn't occur to me that it might have been from Dr. Melrose.... Do you know if it was?"

Lieutenant Randall just said, "We don't know yet."

He went on, "So, after you saw the blood, what did you do?"

"I looked around some more for both Dr. Melrose and Ruthie. I even wondered if the two of them had snuck off somewhere together, believe it or not, maybe to a room upstairs in the hotel for a quickie. But I didn't look very long. I figured Dr. Melrose would be back in the room by then and I had probably missed him somehow. Also, I didn't want to be late if he was going to start the session right after he went back."

"From what we can tell, it was only a couple of minutes at most between the time he returned and when you came in."

Andy didn't quite know what to say. "Yeah, I guess, if you say so. I don't know..."

"When you came into the room, describe what you saw and what happened."

"Well, I told everyone that I hadn't seen Dr. Melrose anywhere, but there was blood on the front edge of the wash basin. Robin Bobbitt was standing there, looking a little weird, and ..."

Lieutenant Randall interrupted him. "Looking a little weird? How?"

"I don't know, and maybe I'm just imagining it in my recollection, but he seemed... what?... a bit pale? Maybe ashy? Maybe a bit bug-eyed? Those aren't right, but he looked different for sure. Maybe he was just in shock."

"Okay, so you saw Dr. Bobbitt, and then?"

"Phillipa seemed to be getting up from the floor. That puzzled me for a split second, but then I looked down and saw Dr. Melrose lying there with the bruise and cut on his forehead and some blood coming from the corner of his mouth. I think I said something like, 'Oh no! What happened?' and then I asked if anyone in the room was a doctor."

He continued, "That man over there said he's a physician."

Andy indicated Dr. Ben Bassett. "He examined the body, but didn't tell us anything we didn't already know, and while that was going on, someone else called 911."

"Phillipa was just getting up from the floor?"

"Yes, she said he didn't have a pulse, so I'm guessing she was down there trying to find a pulse. But that's just a guess. You'll have to ask her."

- - -

Lieutenant Randall called Phillipa over to speak with her again.

"Ms. MaGraw, we're trying to piece things together and need your help here. Let's start with the projection equipment. What happened with that?"

"When I booked the session with the conference, I was told every room would be fully equipped with a computer, projector, and screen – the full system – and that they would have people on hand to explain to the speakers how to use a remote control device to move from slide to slide during their PowerPoint presentations. Yesterday, I looked in at this room to make sure everything was in order, and it seemed to be. Then again at noon today, everything seemed fine with the equipment set up. But then for some bizarre reason, during the supper hour break, the hotel staff removed the equipment from this room and put it in another room where the equipment had broken down during the afternoon.

"I threw a tantrum when I found out what they'd done. They promised to have the equipment put back here right away, but then they were reluctant to interrupt the session going on in the other room..."

"Didn't they need the equipment in that other room, too?" Lieutenant Randall asked.

"Maybe, but I didn't care. They could get the equipment from some other room that wasn't using it, if they had to. The hotel knew very well the equipment wasn't working there, and they had several hours either to get some maintenance geek in there to fix it or to send someone out to get some new equipment. This stuff isn't rocket science, you know. At the very least, they shouldn't have taken it from this room since I had made the point very clearly to them, several times, that we needed it here. Furthermore, they owed us some special consideration; after all, they were going to make a pile of money from the cash bar here and from the hors d'oeuvres we ordered. They owed us."

Lieutenant Randall filed it away: she felt as if once she had done something for someone, she was entitled to some form of reciprocity. Did she feel the same way about Dr. Melrose, and was she upset with him? She'd been working with him for years; was she happy with whatever the arrangement was between them, or was she feeling as if he was short-changing her. From what Lieutenant Randall had learned, it seemed more than just possible that Dr. Melrose had held out on Phillipa somehow, and she could have been upset with him.

"After you threw your tantrum, what took so long for the equipment to arrive and be set up?"

Phillipa spoke very slowly, "*As I said...*" and she glared at them, "The idiots didn't want to interrupt the other session, where they didn't need the projector setup anyway. They didn't want to interrupt them for five measly minutes to remove the equipment and bring it here. Instead they thought it would be just fine to keep this entire room waiting an extra half hour or more. Inconsiderate, unthinking idiots! So I threw another minor tantrum for their benefit. ... Did they ever show up? I was distracted after Dr. Melrose died."

"They arrived shortly after we did," answered Lieutenant Randall. "We sent them away. We'll be needing this room for our investigation, and we'll need several hours to speak with everyone, so I don't think the session will need that equipment now."

"Not with Dr. Melrose dead, we won't," added Phillipa matter-of-factly.

"Just before he left the room, did Dr. Melrose say anything?"

"Yes, he told me he had to use the men's room."

"How did he seem? Did he seem ill or anything?"

"Now that you mention it, I think he had loosened his necktie. And he sort of stumbled a little bit once or twice. It was nothing serious – the kind of thing that can happen to anyone, really, especially someone who is a bit older, like Dr. Melrose. And he hesitated in his speech a bit, too. I wonder if maybe he was unwell. Or maybe the excitement and tension of this evening got to him?"

"How so?"

"As I *told* you, ... this was to be something of a farewell for Dr. Melrose. Also, all the panelists had mentioned that they were not completely on board with his interpretation of their research, and so I think he might have been a bit nervous about that."

Lieutenant Randall suddenly changed gears. "Did Dr. Melrose sleep with any of his patients?"

Phillipa had dealt with these questions before, when the APA was investigating him. "Not that I ever knew of," she lied. "I'm sure you know there was an investigation into those allegations, but it didn't turn up anything."

Phillipa knew. She knew about herself, about Ruthie, and at least two patients. But she was prepared to deny it all completely. She told herself, "I never actually saw them having sex..." but she knew she was covering for him. She also knew there was no good reason to protect his reputation now that he was dead, but she didn't want to have to go into the part-time sexual relationship she'd had with him herself,

123

either. She was embarrassed about it and about not having stood up for herself more and about not having insisted on more respect from Dr. Melrose.

Lieutenant Randall asked her the same question he had asked Dr. Carter earlier, "Would you be surprised to learn that Dr. Melrose had sex with some of his patients?"

Phillipa thought for a moment before answering. Finally, she hedged her answer very carefully, "I really can't say. I suppose anything is possible, though."

Lieutenant Randall sensed that Phillipa wasn't being completely forthcoming, and that sense alone was enough for him. He reminded all the investigators to try to delve into Dr. Melrose's possible history of sexual manipulation and malpractice.

Chapter 17 – **Hors d'oeuvres**

About an hour and a half into the questioning, there was a loud knock on the door, and the hotel staff started to bring several carts filled with hors d'oeuvres into the room. Lieutenant Randall stopped them.

"You can't come in here," he said, showing them his badge and credentials. "Nothing comes in, and nothing goes out."

"What about all this food?" Asked one of the servers.

"Maybe you can just set it up right outside the door," Lieutenant Randall suggested. "That way people who are leaving can help themselves on the way out when we're finished with them."

He called Phillipa over and explained. "I know the food has already been ordered and paid for, but we can't have any other people besides our investigators coming into and going out of this room. I've told the hotel staff to set up the food in the hallway just outside the room so people can help themselves as they're leaving after we're done questioning them."

He thought, but didn't say, "I hope that's alright with you." He didn't have to say that last bit. He had called her over to tell her that, and his having done so was enough of a question in her mind."

Phillipa thought for a moment.

"I don't really see any other options, Lieutenant. You're right, the food was already ordered.; we couldn't possibly cancel that order."

That's what she said but at the same time she was thinking, "What if we tried? What if we said we wouldn't pay because they didn't put it in the room? What if we said we can't pay because Dr. Melrose just died?"

But what she said was, "Oh well, I know Dr. Melrose is dead, but it'll still have to come out of his research funds. The people here might as well be able to eat the food as have it thrown away. If there's any left over after everyone is gone, I hope you and your officers will feel free to help yourselves..."

Lieutenant Randall filed the invitation and continued, "Speaking of his research funds, what will happen to them now that he is dead?"

Again Phillipa paused, "You know, I'm not sure. Maybe Dr. Westover will take over some of his projects..." and she paused... "Or maybe Andy will. ... Hmmm."

And then she continued, "Now that I think about it, Ruthie couldn't possibly take over any of the projects, at least not as they're structured now. Andy might be able to, if he wanted to, but he'd have to find someone here at Jericho State to help him with them..." and she paused just enough that Lieutenant Randall realized she was thinking about offering to help Dr. Kopfmann if he wanted to take on the projects.

"Mostly," she added, "I expect we'll have to use the funds to pay off the expenses of his current projects and wind them down. Whatever funds are left might stay at Jericho State, but some of the funding agencies will insist on a careful auditing and will want whatever is left of their money returned to them."

"What about you? What will you do?"

"I don't know. I'm still in shock. I haven't thought about it at all. ..." She paused for another few seconds and looked at her hands.

Then she looked up and continued, "A number of years ago, Dr. Melrose had me put on a firm university contract, not just a soft money contract that relied on his research grants for funding. So, I'll probably hang around and try to wrap up Dr. Melrose's projects and then see what the university might have in store for me. I don't know, though. I built my life and my work around Dr. Melrose's research consortium. Then again, maybe I'll see if anyone here can offer me a position as good as this one is. Was. Has been."

Lieutenant Randall made a note to check on Phillipa's employment status at Jericho State. If her job depended on Dr. Melrose's continuing grant money, then she'd have less of an incentive to kill him since she would probably lose her job as the funding disappeared. But if she really did have a solid university contract, then she wouldn't have to worry about losing her job if she killed him; she wouldn't necessarily be able to keep her job in the psychology department, but she'd still have a job at Jericho State.

He excused her and met briefly with the other members of his interview team again.

- - -

"What do we have so far?" he asked.

Detective Al Steglitz, one of the investigators, said, "Nothing conclusive. Those four left the room soon after he did, and for all I know, all or none of them had a motive to kill him."

Detective Trudy Newhouse, another of the investigators, joined in, "It's really hard to pin much down right now because we don't know for sure how he died. We don't even know if he was murdered or if he just died from a heart attack or something."

Detective Steglitz nodded. "Yeah, it would really help if we had some idea what we're looking for."

Sergeant Scheffler agreed, "It could have been a heart attack or a stroke. He seemed to be having some problems earlier in the evening, shortly before he left the room to use the restroom – some people mentioned that he stumbled a little, and that his speech was different, but again probably not much, at least not much according to those who knew him very well. Also, he loosened his tie and unbuttoned the top button of his shirt. He could have had a heart attack and fallen against the wash basin and then somehow managed to stagger back here, looking for help."

Detective Newhouse added, "That guy in the plaid coat and bow tie, ..." She checked her notes. "Castman, ... he seemed convinced that Dr. Melrose died of a heart attack or stroke. 'It's classic!' he said.

'The person begins to black out, stumbles, and then staggers somewhere before he dies. And that's probably how he hit his head on the washbasin.' I don't know if that guy knows what he's talking about, but we have to look into it for sure. For all we know, Castman may be trying to cover something up?"

Sergeant Houston nodded in agreement with everything the others said, but what bothered her the most was the plethora of motives – so many people in the room had reasons to dislike Dr. Melrose. She wondered how many disliked him enough to kill him.

"What about motives?" she asked. "There aren't many people in this room who actually liked Dr. Melrose, and there are lots who actively disliked him for one reason or another. Even that guy from Yale, what's his name? Carter? He seemed to bear a grudge of some sort."

Lieutenant Randall said, "You're all right, unfortunately. The most we can say is that the death is a suspicious death, and yet it might have been the result of natural causes. At the same time, we'll have to look into the motives of everyone here in this room and everyone here at this conference. What's worse is that if he was killed by a blow to the head, it could have happened in the men's room by anybody, not just someone here in this room. What a mess!"

"We'll have to wait for the reports from Butts and Holley," he continued, "but let's focus on the likely possible causes of death in this case: natural, including heart attack or stroke, leading to a stumble against the wash basin..."

"We don't even know if that's his blood," Sergeant Scheffler interrupted.

"You're right, of course," replied Lieutenant Randall, "but if it is his, it might have been the result of a heart attack or stroke. That's all I'm saying."

Sergeant Scheffler nodded in agreement.

"But," Lieutenant Randall went on, "if it wasn't natural causes, we have other options to consider. For example, what if someone who left the room slammed his head against the front edge of the wash basin? If that's what happened, it would rule out the women, probably."

"Why?" asked Al Steglitz. "They could have gone in there and smashed his head against the sink, couldn't they?"

"Yes, they could have," answered Lieutenant Randall, "but that would have been taking a big chance. A woman leaving the men's room would have stood out if anyone had been around. But you're right, Steglitz, we can't completely rule them out."

"Here's another variation on that theme." Lieutenant Randall was on a roll and didn't want to be interrupted as he went through the possibilities, thinking out loud. "Someone could have hit Dr. Melrose on the head before he got to the men's room, or after he started leaving it I guess, and then he went back in to clean up a bit and try to recover before he staggered back into the room... It's far-fetched, I know, but again we can't rule it out yet.

"Nuts. I should have thought of this earlier. Patrolman Miller, when we're through talking here, go see hotel security and collect all the surveillance video you can of the hallways on this floor. We want to check on Dr Bobbitt, who said he was wandering the halls while talking on his cellphone; we want to check the movements of Dr. Melrose and see if anyone else entered or left the men's room while he was there; and we want to check on Dr. Kopfmann, too, to see when he went into the men's room and when he left.

"Actually, we need footage for the rest of the hotel, too. We have to check on the other movements of Dr. Kopfmann, and we should try to follow where Dr. Westover and Ms. MaGraw went. Let's hope they have good footage available, including the alley, the loading dock for the kitchen, and the parking areas."

He paused to think where he wanted to go with his meeting, and then he remembered.

"What else might have led to his death that seems even remotely plausible as of now? We have natural causes, blow to the head. And of course there's poison. What else?"

"I don't think he was stabbed or shot," said Sergeant Houston. If he'd been stabbed, there'd have either been a lot of blood or a weapon or something. And if he'd been shot, even with a silenced pistol, wouldn't we have seen a wound or wouldn't someone have seen something?"

"One possibility is that he might have been shot or stabbed in the hallway and then staggered back in here," Lieutenant Randall suggested, "but if he was, we probably should have seen some indication of that... a wound, a blood trail, or something..."

Detective Trudy Newhouse asked, "Is it possible to stab someone through the mouth and into the brain? That might account for the bleeding from his mouth, and maybe the blood in the men's room has nothing to do with the vic."

She thought it sounded cool and big-time to refer to the victim as "the vic".

"Hmmm," said Lieutenant Randall. "Yes, I think it might be possible. Awkward, for sure, but possible. That's worth considering. Butts will be able to tell us. Any other suggestions?"

"Let's not forget that his necktie was *outside* his collar," said Patrolman Miller. "I know Dr. Butts said there were only minor marks on his neck, but they could indicate strangulation, and I don't think we should rule it out."

"Good," said Lieutenant Randall. "Anything else?"

He looked around at each of the members of the investigating team and got no further suggestions.

"So ... here are the things we're looking for and that we're considering:

"If he was poisoned, how? and with what? We need to search the pockets and bags of the people here. Don't let anyone leave, not even the bartenders, without a search. And in case someone tried to dispose of whatever container the poison was in, we need to search the garbage and wastebaskets. And how was the poison administered? Look for needles and other objects. Butts will probably be able to tell us how he was poisoned, if that's it, but we have to search now, here, in this room, and not let any evidence get out of here."

"Did he eat or drink anything that might have been poisoned?" asked Sergeant Scheffler. "Other than the coffee?"

"Get that coffee cup of his," said Lieutenant Randall. "It's marked with his initials. Save it and whatever is still in it for Holly and his gang at forensics."

He looked around. "Anything else?"

Al Steglitz suggested, "Maybe he was poisoned before he got here? I know from nothing about poisons, but aren't there some that take an hour or two before they have any effect?"

"That's possible," Lieutenant Randall nodded. "So another thing we have to do is find out where he was and what he ate before he arrived here, who he was with, everything."

♂♀

Chapter 18 – Dinner and Drinks

The investigators arranged to have some privacy screens delivered to the conference room so they could conduct further interviews and searches with more privacy. They also had the hotel management remove a sliding partition between that conference room and the empty one next to it so they could spread people out a bit more.

"Let's start with the bartenders so they can leave," said Lieutenant Randall, and he called the two of them over.

"We're going to have to search everyone before they leave," he told them, "and after we've talked with you again, you'll be free to go..."

Evan Brook was the older of the two bartenders, sandy-haired, chubby, mid-twenties. "Can you have someone watch the bar and the cash then, please? We can't just leave them unattended."

"It shouldn't be a problem. We'll interview you one at a time so that one of you can always be there, keeping an eye on things."

The interviews with the two bartenders were brief. They went over what the bartenders had seen – it turned out to be nothing different from what everyone else had seen – and the interviewers had the two bartenders empty their pockets. There were some keys and wallets, and Evan had a cigarette lighter, but nothing else.

"Okay, you're free to go now," said Detective Steglitz.

The bartenders went to the portable bar and began wheeling it toward the door.

"Whoa!" shouted Sergeant Scheffler. "What are you doing? You can't take that out of the room!"

"We have to," said Nancy Andrews, the younger of the two bartenders. "We can't leave the room with all the alcohol and cash just sitting here. There's no way to lock things up in this portable bar."

"In that case, you'll have to stay until the end," replied the sergeant. "I'm sorry. I hope you're still on the clock while you're in here. Your boss should understand. If there's a problem with getting paid for your time, let us know, and we'll speak with them."

"Can we at least begin by taking the alcohol and cash and garbage out?"

"Absolutely not. We'll need the garbage for our forensics group for sure, and we may have to take samples from your bottles."

At that point Lieutenant Randall intervened. "We won't need samples from the bottles. If there was poison in one of those, then certainly more than just Dr. Melrose would have been affected."

His eyes went back and forth between the two bartenders. "But Sergeant Scheffler is right. You may not take the garbage or cash or bottles out. If you have to stay here to keep watch over everything, we apologize. Can you pack things up and leave just one of you here? That would be okay with us."

Nancy turned to her co-bartender and said, "Evan, I really need to get some schoolwork done tonight. Would it be okay if you stay and I leave?"

Evan was drifting back and forth between jobs and college and always needed more money.

"Sure," he replied enthusiastically. "I can use all the extra money I can get. I might even get extra for working overtime. Let's split up what we have in tips now, and then I'll keep anything else after this, okay?"

Lieutenant Randall kept an eye on Nancy as she left to make sure she didn't take anything other than her personal belongings with her.

Evan asked, "Is it okay, then, if I keep the bar open? Maybe I can sell a few more drinks and earn a few more dollars in tips..."

Lieutenant Randall hesitated. He didn't want anything to go wrong, and he realized Steglitz might be right about the bottles. What if one of them had been poisoned? He recalled that no one had seen Dr. Melrose have anything to drink other than his coffee, but he didn't want to take any chances.

"Okay, but only beer and wine, and the wine has to come from bottles that haven't been opened yet. Detective Steglitz was right about the opened wine bottles. We'll have to keep those, just in case, until we make sure there's no poison in them."

Lt. Randall used a Sharpie to put Xs on the already opened bottles and had Evan stow them under the bar.

- - -

In the second round of questioning, the interviewers focused on several aspects of the situation: had any of the people there been patients of Dr. Melrose? Had any of them had sex with or been propositioned by Dr. Melrose? Had they been with him or seen him anywhere earlier that evening before the session began? And the investigators paid special attention to what he might have eaten or had to drink before arriving at the room for the session.

It turned out that Dr. Melrose had taken the panelists to dinner at the hotel restaurant before the session.

Robin said, "James was pretty uncreative when it came to ordering dinner. He always had the same, standard meal when he was on an expense account: garden salad, steak done medium-well, *ugh*, potato, and no vegetables; he orders that wherever he goes. But he didn't have any wine with dinner tonight. He told us, 'I'm getting to the age where even a little bit of wine seems to affect me, and I want to stay sharp for the session tonight.'"

Sergeant Houston was questioning Robin. "Who did he sit next to at dinner?

"Let's see... It was just the five of us. I think he made sure he had Ruthie on his right, and I was on his left.

Andy was on the other side of Ruthie and Phillipa was between Andy and me. I tried to snag the seat next to Ruthie, but Andy beat me to it. Actually, it was pretty amusing watching Andy try to talk with Ruthie while Phillipa was trying to talk with him; and meanwhile Ruthie was playing up to James. It was like a giant one-way traffic circle."

"Did you mention the referral fees to Dr. Melrose at dinner?"

"No, and I wish I had. Actually, I wanted to, but the conversations didn't really seem to make room for me to raise the subject with him, and it never seemed to fit in. But as I said, I wish I had confronted him then instead of blurting it all out here in the conference room."

"Did you notice anything unusual about anyone's behavior during dinner?"

"Nothing that stands out. Given who we are and what we study, it all seemed pretty normal. There was lots of sexual and academic tension, but as I said, that's pretty normal for us. Ruthie was cozying up to James to work on getting the endowed chair she has her eye on, Andy was trying to rekindle an affair with Ruthie, Phillipa was desperately trying strike up any kind of relationship she could with Andy."

"What about you? And what about Dr. Melrose?"

"I kept trying to butt into Ruthie's conversations with Dr. Melrose. Ruthie's a very exciting woman to be with – you can see that – and I wanted to chat her up some. Put bluntly, I was hoping to emerge as the dominant male tonight and win the prize of going home with her. But also, I guess I had some desire to put James down because he was stiffing me for those referral fees. ... Hmmm... Maybe I'll send an invoice to his estate..."

"And Dr. Melrose?"

"He was clearly enjoying the attention from Ruthie. And I think my interjections irritated him in part because he didn't want me to interrupt the fawning all over him that she was doing and in part because he didn't want to deal with the issue of the referral fees. It was the first time we had met face-to-face since we made our agreement, and I think he didn't want to be confronted about his reneging on the deal."

"How was the bill settled?"

"Oh, James made it clear when he invited us that his research grants from the SGA Foundation were going to cover the dinner. I think he put the tab on his business credit card."

"Think carefully now... Did you see anyone touch his food, his plate, his salad bowl, his water, his coffee or anything?"

"Wow! You mean he might have been poisoned?"

"We can't rule anything out at this point, so we have to ask about every possibility."

Robin responded slowly. "All I saw was that when we toasted to his health, he and Ruthie clinked glasses – his water glass with her wine glass. I don't remember anything other than that. He did stop at one point to take some medication with his water, but I don't think anyone else was involved then."

"Medication?"

"He called them his 'placebos'... some supplements he takes, hoping they'll keep him healthy. Glucosamine is one but I have no idea what the others are... were... vitamins, I suppose. Hunh! Probably Viagra or Cialis or something."

- - -

Sergeant Houston relayed this information to Lieutenant Randall who said, "Dr. Butts will examine his stomach contents to be make certain, but maybe someone slipped something into his pill collection at dinner time somehow? She said she'll do a full tox screen, too. Let's make sure we get Bob Holly to check whatever is left in Dr. Melrose's pockets in case there are other indications he was poisoned at dinnertime."

The others who were at the dinner confirmed what Robin said, but with different nuances to reflect their own personal interests. They all had different slants, interpretations, and very personal perspectives.

When Sergeant Scheffler interviewed her a second time, Ruthie said, "I wanted to keep the conversations with James positive during dinner to get his support for my promotion. I knew I would be disagreeing with his research results later during our panel presentations and discussions, and I wanted to soften the effects of those disagreements by being positive with him at dinner."

She added, "I think I did a pretty good job of it, despite the fact that AndyBoy over there kept interrupting me and kept sliding closer to me, trying to touch my leg with his. I was so over him and so done with him, but he wouldn't take 'no' for a put down. I had to be rude to him several times, but he acted as if he thought we were just engaged in some sort of verbal foreplay. Geez, what a loser.

"And Robin kept interrupting, too. He was after me, but he also had some sort of beef with James. I didn't discover what that was about until he blurted it out here, in this room, that he had been referring patients to James in exchange for referral fees."

"Did you ever offer anything to Dr. Bobbitt in exchange for referrals?" asked Sergeant Scheffler.

"That's disgusting! Are you implying I offered to sleep with him to get referrals?"

"Did you?"

"No!"

"But you did have a lengthy relationship with him when he was a graduate student, and he was trying to renew that at least for tonight?"

"Yes, and yes, but get this! ..." She seemed pretty angry. "I wanted nothing more to do with Rob Bob. Furthermore, my private practice is more than bursting at the seams. I have more patients than I can handle. I don't need to offer *anything* to get more clients. You got that?!"

"We'll certainly want to look at your client administrative files to confirm it," replied Sergeant Scheffler, not letting her attitude intimidate him.

Phillipa and Andy told pretty much the same stories. Andy was frustrated about not having had a chance to talk with Ruthie as much as he wanted, and Phillipa felt left out of the conversations. She said something like, "Oh Robin and Andy talked with me some at dinner, but they were both more interested in carrying on with Ruthie."

Overall, it seemed unlikely, though not impossible, that Dr. Melrose had been poisoned during dinner.

♂♀

Chapter 19 – **Wrapping Up?**

The more he thought about it, the more Lieutenant Randall wanted to focus on Dr. Melrose's coffee as a likely source of poison. ... if he was poisoned.

It was after midnight when they finished questioning and searching everyone. As each person was let go, they were told, "You're free to go, but don't leave town for the next day or two. And be sure to help yourself to some of the hors d'oeuvres out there in the hallway as you leave."

Dr. Carter complained, "I have classes to meet tomorrow afternoon at Yale. My flight leaves Chicago from Midway Airport at noon."

"I'll have to ask you to change your flight and stick around for another day," said Lieutenant Randall, writing the incident number on the back of one of his business cards. "Tell the airline the circumstances, and they'll change your flight, no charge."

"But what about my classes?"

"Don't tell me you've never canceled a class on short notice before, Doctor. And don't tell me the students won't be happy to put it off until later."

"I suppose you're right. If you insist..."

"We'll let you know if the situation changes and you can leave earlier."

Lieutenant Randall wasn't too concerned about letting Dr. Carter go after another interview the next day. So far as he could tell, there were no major gripes between Drs. Carter and Melrose. It didn't look as if they had had but a brief moment of talking together, and from all reports, Dr. Melrose had left his coffee at the head table while he was talking with Dr. Carter.

Andy Kopfmann presented more of a problem.

"I'm booked on an overnight flight out of O'Hare the day after tomorrow," he said. "I can't miss that flight."

"You may have to," replied Lieutenant Randall. "Once you're out of the US, we'd have a dickens of a time getting you back here, so we're not letting you leave Illinois until we're certain you had nothing to do with the death of Dr. Melrose. I strongly advise you to get on the phone with the airline and your ticketing agent to move your departure date back a day or three."

"That'll be expensive!" Andy complained. "I can't afford to pay more to change my flight. And I can't afford to stay here in the hotel any longer."

"Relax. The airlines understand about these things. They're unlikely to charge you any extra to change your flight. Give them my number and this incident number," and he handed Andy his business card on which he wrote 'Case #4VJ69ASP'.

Andy took the card and wandered over to Phillipa.

"Phillipa, do you think Dr. Melrose's grant will cover an extra night or two at this hotel if I have to stay longer to answer more questions from the police?"

Phillipa was disappointed. When she saw him walking toward her, she knew he'd been asked to stay in town, and she hoped he would ask to stay with her.

She lied to him. "I don't think so. We'll face serious audits if we pay for extensions beyond the dates of the conference," and she looked at him hopefully.

"Oh," was all Andy said.

"I have a pull-out sofa, though. Why don't you come and stay at my place?"

Andy hesitated. He knew he wouldn't be able to resist ending up in bed with Phillipa if he went there. He thought to himself, "How will I feel tomorrow morning? ... She's nice. ... And she doesn't look like that evil neighbor we had when I was growing up... and she really has been very nice to me ... Who knows? This might be a good idea ... Well, here goes..."

"That'd be great! Thanks!" he smiled.

Phillipa couldn't believe it. She quickly slung her shoulder bag over her right shoulder and put her left hand through Andy's right arm. She couldn't wait to get him home.

Nearly half of the others were also from out of state. Lieutenant Randall told each of them "Don't leave town tomorrow. And check with us before you leave town the day after tomorrow. We'll try to have word for you as soon as we can. ... and be sure to help yourself to some of the hors d'oeuvres."

Before they were released, Ruthie tried Dr. Carter again. "Well, Dwayne, are you ready to go for that drink now?"

He thought to himself, 'It might be fun for now, but I don't need this.'

"I'd love to, but I really must get to work on those student papers, and all this questioning by the police has really cut into the time I was counting on for grading."

"But aren't they making you stay here another night? You'll have all day tomorrow to grade your papers! C'mon..."

"Dr. Westover," he said, using a formal tone to discourage her, "they do want me to stay, but I'm hopeful that things will be resolved quickly, for me at least. There's a good chance the Medical Examiner will determine James died of a heart attack or a stroke or something, and if that's the case, I'm leaving as soon as possible."

Ruthie wasn't deterred. She put her hand on his arm, partly to ward off unwanted attentions from Andy, Robin, Roddie Castman, and several others. She also wanted to see if she could possibly warm Dr. Carter up enough to interest him in changing his mind. She didn't take rejection easily.

It didn't work, though. Dr. Carter turned away from her and said, "If you'll excuse me, I need to stop at the next men's room now – before I try to make it to the elevator." He hurried past the men's room that was still closed to the public with crime-scene tape and a posted guard.

Ruthie stood in the hallway, frustrated, but accepting defeat. She wasn't going to embarrass herself by waiting for Dr. Carter outside a men's room. As she walked slowly toward the elevator, she saw Robin waiting there along with Roddie Castman.

"Well, look who's here!" smiled Roddie. "Why don't we all go down to the bar to unwind? This is all really new to me, and..." he almost leered at Ruthie, "... it really does fire me up somehow. I really could use something to tame that inner fire right now."

Robin was tired, and he had a full day ahead of him at his recording studio. He would have welcomed a quick bedding with Ruthie, but he knew he'd have to outwait Roddie to even have a chance of that. "Besides," he thought, "It'll do Ruthie some good to have to accept her sixteenth choice for the night."

"You two go ahead," he said. "I need to turn in."

Ruthie hesitated. Did she want to end up with Roddie? She looked at him for a moment and then she smiled, "Sure! Let's do it!"

He could hardly contain his excitement.

Her plan was to let him pay for the drinks, which he gladly did. Then she slowly worked into being as seductive as she could. 'I'll show this yokel a time he'll never forget,' she thought. It was all about her being in control and having the power to leave men wanting even more from her.

And that's what happened. He was begging her not to leave when she got dressed and left his hotel room to go home at 4am that morning.

"Thanks for the drinks, Roddie, and the fun; but that was it. Go home and cherish the memories. *And don't call me!*"

♂♀

Chapter 20 – **Means, Motive, and Opportunity**

After all the guests were cleared and had left the room, Lieutenant Randall encouraged the investigators to help themselves to whatever hors d'oeuvres were left on the tables in the hallway.

"When we spoke earlier, Ms. MaGraw was insistent that we should help ourselves to whatever is left," he said, "so have what you'd like now and feel free to take some of the leftovers home with you."

Then he asked Evan, the bartender, if he could buy a round of drinks for the investigators.

"On the house," said Evan with a smile.

Steglitz and Newhouse opted for wine while the rest asked for Starved Rock Beer from one of the local breweries. Sergeant Houseman asked for club soda though.

"What gives?" asked Sergeant Scheffler. "You usually have a beer. You'd be okay to drive after one, you know that."

"I'm pregnant," she said as she smiled broadly. "I wasn't going to announce it yet, but I can't hold it in any longer."

After all the congratulations, hugs, hearty-blue macho backslaps, and queries about her due date, they all took their drinks to the head table. With the drinks poured, Evan asked if he could pack up the portable bar and leave.

"Okay," answered Lieutenant Randall, "but don't take any of the garbage with you. We'll need to keep that. And help yourself to some of the food out in the hallway, if there's any left."

- - -

While the others were moving some chairs to the head table and getting settled for their retro-recap session, Lieutenant Randall excused himself to call home.

"The problem is," he told Louise, "we don't know if he died of natural causes or something else, so we have to consider everything."

They groaned together.

"When might you be able to get home?"

"We're about to do our retro here at the site, then I'll have to write up my report. I can do that at home, though, so I shouldn't be more than another hour or so."

There were seven investigators still on the scene, sitting around the table: Randall at one end, with Scheffler, Houston, and Newhouse down one side, and Miller, Keene, and Steglitz down the other.

Lieutenant Randall began. "Let's keep in mind that Dr. Melrose may have died from natural causes. We have no clear evidence of anything else yet. Dr. Butts will let me know as soon as she has something. So will Bob Holly and the lab people."

"Why are speculating, then?" asked Detective Newhouse. "Why don't we wait until we have their reports?"

"There are at least two good reasons for these retros," answered Lieutenant Randall. "Sergeant Houston, you go first."

She smiled. She'd worked with Lieutenant Randall long enough that she anticipated his turning the questions back to his sergeants.

"By discussing everything together," she began, "We can try to make sure we don't overlook any of the possibilities. If it was murder, we don't want to let any of these people leave town until they're cleared. Oops, maybe that's two."

Lieutenant Randall nodded. "Sergeant Scheffler?"

He scratched his left arm, pretending to think, but he knew the answer and had it ready. "Sometimes in these retro sessions, we come up with information and connections that help us provide some additional guidance for Dr. Butts and Bob Holly. I mean, I know Dr. Butts will check to see if he's diabetic, but if one of us here at the table had a witness or could tell us if he had some other health condition, it would be good to know."

"Or," he continued, "maybe three or four of us heard different things that will fit together when we share them all like this, when they're fresh. You know how it can go sometimes: you heard A from X, I heard B from Y, and the lieutenant heard C from Z. A plus B plus C will all go together to help us pinpoint the murderer, if that's what it was, but we can't tell that until we discuss it, especially if it's buried in our written reports, assuming it makes it there at all."

Lieutenant Randall added, "Exactly, and you still need to write up your reports! And it'll take a while because we have so many people and so many options to cover. However, until then..."

He swallowed some beer.

"What are the likeliest options if it wasn't natural causes?"

Patrolman Keene offered, "Well, poison is an obvious possibility, but I have no idea what kind of poison would work like that or how it might have been done..."

"Good. We'll address what type and how in a minute," said Lieutenant Randall. "How else might he have died?"

"It's probably a long shot," said Detective Steglitz, "but his tie was outside his collar, and his neck had some marks on it. And Dr. Butts didn't rule out strangulation."

"Okay. Anything else?"

Patrolman Miller asked, "Could someone have caught him from behind and slammed his head against the wash basin? You know, death by blunt force trauma?"

"We can't rule it out."

"Check to see if he'd been sexually active recently," suggested Sergeant Houston. "Judging from what everyone was saying about her, Ruthie could have ... um ... you know ... um ... done him to death."

They all burst into laughter, but Lieutenant Randall calmed them quickly by saying in slightly skeptical tone of voice, "You're right that energetic sex in a man his age might have caused a heart attack, but it seems unlikely here. Either the heart attack would have had to happen with a delay if they had sex after dinner but before the session, or she'd have had to go into the men's room with him for a quickie. We'll want to check the security videos for sure to see if she went in there. I don't think we could rule that murder, though, if that's what happened. Maybe negligent homicide?" he laughed.

Someone started singing, "Killing him softly, with her love..." and they all continued to smile or chuckle.

Lieutenant Randall got them back on track by saying very seriously, "We'll have Dr. Butts check for recent sexual activity if she doesn't do that automatically, but I think it's a standard part of her routine."

Patrolman Miller asked, "The videos will also help maybe rule out anyone else from the rest of the hotel, too, won't they? And they might show if anyone from this session entered or left the men's room with anything that could have been used as a weapon?"

He was making suggestions, but he was ending them up in the air as if they were questions because he hadn't been a part of a murder investigation before. He wanted to be noticed as someone who could contribute meaningfully, but he also wanted to defer to the senior investigators. He didn't want to seem too aggressive or too ambitious.

"The videos will certainly help, depending on how thorough and detailed they are. Let's keep our fingers crossed about the video files. Miller, before you leave, make sure you get every single security tape or disk or whatever they use, covering mid-afternoon onward."

"Done, sir. They keep the video files on their security computer hard drive. I've emailed the files to headquarters and I've had copies of them transferred to a USB stick. It's here in my bag. And I've told the hotel not to erase those files until we say they can."

"Excellent. Good work. So, poison, strangulation, blunt force trauma, and sex are the likely causes of death if wasn't a natural cause..."

Lieutenant Randall went on. "Given what everyone has said so far, we don't want to rule out anything, but it's looking as if poison was the most likely cause of death if it wasn't due to natural causes. Okay, if it was poison, how was it administered?"

Trudy Newhouse thought to herself, 'What's with this guy? Why is he asking us to do his thinking for him? Is he incompetent, or is he just trying to make us feel included? She decided to decide later, hoping it was some of both.'

She didn't have long to wait.

"We don't want to overlook *any* possibilities," Lieutenant Randall added in a speech Trudy hadn't heard before but that was part of his post-mortem retro routine. "I'm not likely to think of everything, and neither is any one of you, so let's hear your ideas so we can pool our thoughts and try to anticipate things."

Sergeant Houston began. "We pretty much ruled out anyone poisoning his food or beverages at dinner. Not completely, I know, but those seem unlikely."

Sergeant Scheffler added, "And once we get the reports, we should be able to tell whether somebody substituted some sort of poison pill for one of his supplements that he took at dinner. But I think dinner is a low-prob time for it to have happened. If it was poison, we'll have to think about whatever might have happened after he got to this room."

Lieutenant Randall nodded and then asked him, "So how might the poison have been given to him here, in this room?"

Sergeant Scheffler was ready for it. "Not one person in the room saw him drink or eat anything here except his coffee. Good thing we saved that for analysis."

"Probably," added Patrolman Keene, "but didn't Dr. Butts also note a small pin prick or nick or something on the side of the victim's neck? In all the hubbub and commotion in the room, could someone have injected him with some poison?"

"Excellent," replied Lieutenant Randall. "Anything else?" He was pleased with the work of both the Patrolmen.

"Let's not rule out dinner and those pills," said Sergeant Houston. "Maybe he got some of his medications mixed up at home and it was an accidental poisoning."

"Good," said Lieutenant Randall. "Anything else?"

They sat and looked at each other but no one could think of any other way someone might have poisoned Dr. Melrose.

"Okay." Lieutenant Randall carried on, "Setting the possibility of poison aside for a moment, I'm guessing that if he was killed by strangulation or slamming his head onto the wash basin, the security videos will pretty much help us."

He turned to Gerald Miller and said, "Once again, let me commend you for arranging to get the security videos, Miller. I expect they will come in handy. If we see the action on the video, or if we see only one person go into the men's room while Dr. Melrose was in there, then we'll have things narrowed down pretty well, won't we?"

Detective Trudy Newhouse spoke up, "When did Dr. Kopfmann go into the men's room? Did he go in before or after Dr. Melrose came back out?"

Lieutenant Randall replied, "Good. He *said* he went in and Dr. Melrose wasn't in there, so, if he's telling the truth, he went in after Dr. Melrose had already left. Again, Miller's video should be able help us out with this."

"Let's talk about motives," he continued. "Apparently the good doctor wasn't very well liked but was tolerated, if not respected, by most of the people who were here. Let's take the possibles one at a time, beginning with Phillipa MaGraw. Sergeant Scheffler?"

"She liked her job, and she respected him in lots of ways. Three-to-one they had slept together at some point in their past. She had a temper, too, according to the people in the room. They all talked about how she went overboard, chewing out the hotel staff."

"But did she have a motive for killing him?" asked the lieutenant.

"I can think of two, and they probably go together," replied Sergeant Scheffler. "First, anger, and second, jealousy. If Dr. Melrose had been bedding her but was playing up to Dr. Westover, that might have pushed Ms. MaGraw over the edge. From what people said, I wouldn't want to get her mad at me... but if it was poison, it wasn't a crime of passion. It was well-planned. We'll have to see if there was some ongoing, underlying problem between them that might have led her to plan to poison her boss. From what we heard tonight from the others about her, it's possible."

Lieutenant Randall looked at Sergeant Houston next. "What about Dr. Kopfmann?"

She replied, "Two motives for him as well. First, he wanted to shack up with Dr. Westover for the night, but she was apparently really playing up to Dr.

Melrose, especially at dinner. I know, she later shifted to Dr. Carter, and so if it was jealousy, maybe he'd have gone after her, not Dr. Melrose. But couple that jealousy with the other thing – he seemed upset that Dr. Melrose was misrepresenting his research. What did he say to someone? 'He can't keep doing that. He's destroying my career.' That sounds strong enough to be a motive."

"Yes," added Detective Newhouse, "Dr. Kopfmann seemed jealous of him, not just because Dr. Westover was playing up to him, but also because he had power and authority over Dr. Kopfmann. After all, it was Dr. Melrose who paid for his trip here from Liechtenstein, and Dr. Melrose who helped him with grants while he was doing his research in Vancouver and Vietnam. Sometimes when someone owes another person a lot, they become resentful, especially if it's someone like Dr. Melrose who seems like the kind of man who would lord it over you and try to make you feel obligated to him forever."

"Good," said Lieutenant Randall. He turned to Detective Steglitz, "What about Dr. Bobbitt?"

"He may have had a motive, but it seems pretty weak to me," said the detective. "Probably two motives, actually, like Dr. Kopfmann. Jealousy, for sure. He wanted to end up with Dr. Westover for the night and he seemed to have some serious residual resentment about their breakup years ago. He may be the type who has trouble letting things go, like the referral fees Dr. Melrose had promised him. That's the other motive. Both of his motives would come from resentment and a desire for revenge."

"I talked with him some," added Patrolman Miller. "He certainly had that edge to him. Also, even though he felt an obligation to Dr. Melrose for having gotten him into and through graduate school, he also felt as if Dr. Melrose looked down on him and disrespected him for having a PhD from that place out west. Even though Dr. Bobbitt knew that his PhD was of questionable merit, he didn't like being put down because of it all the time, and Dr. Melrose kept doing that to him."

"Okay, Detective Newhouse, what about Dr. Westover?"

"Oh, she had motive enough. If Scheffler gives three-to-one that MaGraw had been sleeping with the vic, I'll give thirty-to-one that Westover was. I know someone who was a patient of hers.... Don't ask, not me! ... I'll talk to them again, but the impression I got was that she uses sex, not just sex appeal, to get everything."

"What does that mean for this case?" asked Lieutenant Randall.

"It's pretty straight-forward, I should think. She'd slept with Dr. Melrose to get where she was, and she thought she could do it some more to get that promotion we heard she wanted. Quite possibly, he was accepting the sexual favors she was providing, but he was holding out on the promotion. That would have really upset her. It was a blow to her femininity; I'd say it was an unwanted challenge to her own perception of herself as irresistible. Beyond that, she may have thought that with Dr. Melrose out of the way, her chances of getting that promotion would be better. And from what I heard, it's easy to imagine

159

he'd hold out on her as long as possible, trying for more sex along the way."

Lieutenant Randall looked around the table. "This is good so far. Any other suspects we should consider?"

Without waiting for an answer, he went on, "What about Dr. Carter, that dream guy from Yale? We need to try to rule him out, if he didn't do it, so he can leave town. Same thing for the others who are here from out of town: Murphy, McBride, Castman, any others?

Patrolman Keene spoke up. "Well, Murphy said he didn't know any of these people. I can follow up on that."

Lieutenant Randall checked his notes. "Murphy isn't leaving until two days from now. McBride, like many of the women in the room, had eyes for Dr. Bobbitt."

That response seemed to bother Patrolman Keene, but he slipped past it quickly and the others were gracious enough to the newcomer to let it slide. He continued, "I don't think she had ever had any contact or anything with the vic."

Like Newhouse, he liked using the expression 'the vic'; it made him feel as if he was a real investigator, like the ones on television, and not just a beat cop.

"And Castman's a joke," said Detective Steglitz. "From what people said, he hit on every woman in the room, but he was especially interested in Dr. Westover. He might have killed Dr. Melrose to eliminate some competition, but he'd have had to kill Dr. Carter, too."

And then he half-laughed as he added, "What is this, PBS's Animal Kingdom where the males kill off all their rivals?"

Lieutenant Randall ignored the question.

"Here are some assignments," he said. "First, and this is really important, keep your smartphones charged up so I can email or text anything else we think of. I won't text you until after eight in the morning, so after we're done here, go write up your reports and then get some sleep. It's going to be a long day tomorrow.

"Keene and Miller, I'm keeping you two with me for now. You're on garbage duty tonight. Take those two bags of garbage back to headquarters now, then write up your reports while you're there. Get Hanson – I think he's on desk tonight – get him to set you up with the forms you'll need for your reports and to help you find a room to put the garbage in. Then get hold of Bobby Holly and have him send some people there from forensics first thing tomorr ..."

He stopped and looked at his watch.

"Nope this morning... We want forensics to go through the garbage with a fine-toothed comb, looking for anything that might have contained poison.

"In the morning, start by seeing Dr. Butts at the M.E.'s office and get Melrose's personal effects. Go through them to find his next of kin or to see if there's anyone listed in his wallet that he wanted notified in case of an emergency. I didn't see anything when I looked earlier, but that was just a quick look. If you don't find anything there, call Ms. MaGraw; she might very likely know who his personal lawyer is, where his will is, and all that.

"Also, you two have the unenviable chore of notifying the next of kin. Don't try to slide that responsibility off onto a lawyer or Ms. MaGraw. Do it yourselves. In person if they're in town, or by telephone otherwise. You may have to look through his personal files somewhere to find out who it is, or maybe the lawyer can tell you when you find out who that is.

"Once you've done that, or maybe as part of it, take his keys and go to his home. If there's no one there, go in and look around. Pay special attention to his medications; collect them and bring them in just in case we need them for analysis.

"And find his will – see his lawyer or executor and see who inherits. Then follow up on those leads. That's a lot, so you'll probably have to divide it up. I'll leave it to you two to decide who does what."

"What about our regular duties?" asked Patrolman Miller. "Who's gonna cover for us?"

"Don't worry about that. I'll get a message to the Chief right now and he can look after it."

He quickly two-finger-typed an email and then carried on with his assignments.

"Newhouse, you follow up with Westover. You have her address, right? And where she can be reached at Guthrie Hall if she's not at home in the morning? Try to find out more about whether she might have had any reasons other than the ones we've mentioned to want Melrose out of the way. And try to find out more about those possibilities."

"Yes, sir."

"Steglitz, you get Bobbitt. You may have to follow him around a bit to keep up with him, but start at his home in the morning, and if you have to, go with him to the studio where he records his programs. Push him more on his apparent need for revenge. Maybe even speak with the people he works with. See if you can get them to talk about how vengeful he could be.

"Houston, Kopfmann is yours. Make sure he doesn't leave town, for a start, and push him some more on motives. What's he doing in Liechtenstein? Why is he there? Did anything go wrong in Vancouver? Did Dr. Melrose actually interfere with his career because he wouldn't support Melrose's work? If so, how? Does he have an ongoing relationship with anyone?

"And Scheffler, MaGraw is yours. She might be a frustrated middle-aged single woman, or maybe she isn't. Check on her personal relationships. And check with others in the psychology department at Jericho State to learn more about her relationship with Dr. Melrose – did she ever roll her eyes behind his back? make derogatory remarks about him? anything."

"And one more thing," he reminded them all, "Do your reports before you go to bed tonight, and don't skimp. The worst thing you can do is say, 'Oh, that's not important, I don't need to include that.' or 'I'll remember that.' I recommend the speech-to-text app we should all have on our phones by now. It'll cut your time to a third or less than what it would take to type everything, so you'll be more thorough that way."

Chapter 21 – **The Process of Elimination**

Mike Randall got home at 1:30 that morning, and Louise had some hot water ready to make him some instant decaf coffee.

"Lou," he said, "It's a mess. Four major suspects, and they all have motives, but we can't figure much out until we get the reports from Doc Butts and Bobby Holly."

"How long will that take?" she asked.

"I don't know. We should have some preliminary stuff from the doc by morning, but with Holly you never know; some of those tests he runs can take a few days..."

"But here's something else," he said. "Sergeant Houston is pregnant. I'm..."

"That's wonderful!" said Louise.

"Not for me, it isn't," complained Mike. "I've just trained her up nicely and she was doing very well as a sergeant; now she'll be off on maternity leave. Why do women have to have babies, anyway?"

Louise glared at him, and then she laughed with just a hint of scorn. "Don't be silly, Mike."

- - -

At 2am, he was seated at the dining room table, working away on his laptop editing the report he had dictated when he got an email from Dr. Butts.

Hey Mike,
It probably wasn't natural causes. No sign of a heart attack, no sign of a stroke. No indication he was diabetic. We'll look some more, but I don't think we'll find anything.

Also, those marks around his neck? They were just chafing from wearing starched collars. Who uses starch in collars anymore? Sheesh.

And that neck nick? Nothing there. Probably cut himself while shaving.

And to answer the big question, no he had not been sexually active recently.

Stomach contents: salad, steak, potatoes, coffee. The smell seemed just a bit unusual, so we've sent the contents off to Holly for analysis. I'm guessing poison of some kind. Not sure what.

We've taken some blood samples and sent them out for a full tox screen. No idea when we'll get 'em back.

I hear you all got drinks on the house before you left. You owe me a glass of wine.

Julie

Mike replied,

> Thanks, Doc. Next time we're offered drinks on the house, I'll text you to drop what you're doing and stop by.
>
> Mike

He had promised his team he wouldn't text them before 8am, and he didn't want to wake them with a text at 2am, and so he sent out short emails to them:

> Prelim ME report: Almost surely poison. Continue as planned.

After setting his alarm for 8am so he could get up and see their three kids before they left for school, Mike finished editing his report and went to bed. After the kids were out the door the next morning, he showered, shaved and went to the office, arriving by 9am.

Bob Holly's assistants from forensics were already there, on the job, going through the garbage from the night before. He commended them on their promptness and told them, "Let me know the minute you come up with anything suspicious. We got a prelim from the M.E. last night that it's probably poison, so pay special attention to anything that might have been poison or might have held some poison."

Miller texted him to let him know that there was no information about the next of kin in Dr. Melrose's wallet, and so they were taking his keys and going to his home. They left everything else with Dr. Butts' group to box up for forensics.

- - -

Sergeant Scheffler arrived at the psychology department in Guthrie Hall at Jericho State just a little after 9am to begin making his inquiries about Phillipa.

"Oh, she called in sick about half an hour ago," said Alice Carpenter, the department administrator. "Was Dr. Melrose really killed at that conference last night? Gosh, that'll be so hard on Phillipa. She lived for him and her job with him. She'll need a few days of compassionate leave for sure."

Sergeant Scheffler was non-committal. "Well, he died there last night, but we still aren't certain about how he died. The Medical Examiner hasn't filed her report, yet."

He changed pace. "Do you know of anyone who might have had a grudge against him?"

Alice frowned, and then she took a sheet of paper from her desk drawer. "Here. This is a list of everyone in the department, faculty and graduate students. I don't think there's a person on that list who didn't have some sort of gripe about him. But kill him? I don't know... I doubt it."

"Thanks. May I keep this?"

Alice nodded, and with a serious but sarcastic edge, she added, "You may want get a complete list of everyone who was ever a student or office employee here, too."

He noted that and then continued, "I want to ask about the relationship between Phillipa and Dr. Melrose. What can you tell me about it?"

"They were together for a long time... at least twenty years, I think," she said. "Phillipa started with him before I came here."

"How did they get along?"

"From what I heard, she started out worshipping him, but from what I've seen she ended up mothering him and running his life for him."

"What does that mean?"

"Well, when I first got here, they seemed closer in a different kind of way, if you get my drift. There were rumors that they were sleeping together, but if they were, it wasn't on a regular, monogamous basis. He tried to bed every woman he met. ... and he bragged in not very subtle ways about his conquests. When he tried it with me, I 'accidentally' stabbed him with a pencil and glared at him. He never bothered me again."

Alice added with a glint of a smile and determination, "If he was stabbed to death last night, check *all* the women who were there."

"Did Ms. MaGraw say or even hint at anything in the past month or so that might have indicated the two of them had had a falling out?"

"Nothing I can think of ... There was this, though. It was obvious to everyone that Phillipa was *really* looking forward to the visit by Andy Kopfmann. She didn't actually gush over him when he was a student here, but she was clearly interested in him then, and I don't think that flame ever died out. She couldn't stop talking about him during the past week.

"I can't pinpoint anything, but I don't think Dr. Melrose was ever very happy about her interest in Andy. It was as if he felt he owned her or something. Mind you, it was never anything he said or did that you could put your finger on; it was just that he seemed to behave that way toward her."

"You mean he thought it was okay for him to have numerous partners but not for her?"

"That's a pretty blunt way of saying it, but yeah I guess so."

- - -

Sergeant Scheffler thanked Alice and drove to visit Phillipa at her home, a two-bedroom apartment on the 8th floor of a high rise building about two and a half miles from the Jericho State campus.

When he buzzed her unit from the lobby, she replied, "I'm really not ready to see anyone this morning. Can you come back this afternoon or tomorrow?" and she disconnected.

He buzzed her again, "I'll have to insist, Ms. MaGraw," and he wondered what it meant for her not to be ready.

The answer was clear when he got to her apartment. Andy Kopfmann was still in the shower, and Phillipa was flushed. He couldn't tell whether she was flushed from embarrassment, sexual activity, or romantic glow.

"Come on in, Sergeant," she said, and she added a little too matter-of-factly. "Andy's in the shower right now, but he'll be out soon."

Sergeant Scheffler decided not to ask about her having phoned in sick, assuming that she was using that as an excuse to spend the day with Dr. Kopfmann before he returned to Liechtenstein. Instead he excused himself briefly and went into her kitchen, where he texted Sergeant Houston with a cc to Lieutenant Randall.

> Kopfmann is with MaGraw. Apparently spent night. Want to join me here?

Lieutenant Randall texted back,

> Scheffler, you interview both.
>
> Houston, get on to the van and limo services to O'Hare and the airlines that fly to Liechtenstein and tell them not to let either Kopfmann or MaGraw board them without checking with us first. Then go see Castman and Carter at the hotel for follow-ups.

Sergeant Scheffler texted back, "Got it," and Sergeant Houston texted, "Yes, sir."

While Dr. Kopfmann was dressing, Sergeant Scheffler took a seat in one of the matching pale green wingback chairs in Phillipa's living room.

"Are you and Dr. Kopfmann in a relationship?"

She answered very matter-of-factly, "I'd like to be, but this was our first night together."

"Are you planning to travel with him soon?"

"I would if he wanted me to. I can afford it, and I'm due a few months of accumulated vacation time. But he hasn't asked, and I'd appreciate it you don't mention it to him... at least not while I'm around today. Let me pick the right time to suggest it."

"Sure. Ms. MaGraw, did you and Dr. Melrose have a sexual relationship?"

She grimaced. "Okay... Last night I denied it. But yes, when he first hired me, I worshiped the man. And we slept together now and then. But as the worship factor diminished, I still loved my job with him, and I loved running his life for him. I had no reason to want to him dead."

"Were you jealous of his other relationships?"

"At first, yes, of course; but eventually I got over it. Even though we slept together now and then after that, I knew it was something temporary and fleeting..."

At that point Andy walked into the room and Phillipa stopped talking. She smiled at Andy and then looked at Sergeant Scheffler as if to say, "Time to move on to a new topic."

Sergeant Scheffler greeted Andy nonchalantly, as if there was no reason to be surprised, and then turned back to Phillipa. "Ms. MaGraw, how would you describe your relationship with Dr. Melrose for the past three or four years? I know you worked with and for him for over twenty years, but I'd like you to focus on just the last three or four years, okay?"

"I think we respected each other in many ways. He could be a domineering s.o.b. sometimes, but then I had developed into quite the control freak myself. I loved running his life: the life of the man who had been my professor and my mentor and who had given me this wonderful opportunity to be involved in everything. I think, too, he had pretty much given up on trying to dominate me because he knew I looked after so many details for him. He tried, and he talked like a boss, but he knew I ran things for him.

"And yet he had an enormous ego that I had to work with. I had to figure out ways to get around it, and over the years, I did, so we got along pretty well. He thought he had power, and I guess he did in some ways, but I had more power than I'd ever had in my life."

She faked a demure smile, "I liked it."

"Have you thought any more about what will happen to your job now that Dr. Melrose is dead?"

"As I told you last night, I have a university appointment. I've had it for over ten years now, and so they'll have to give me the first chance to apply for

173

other jobs on campus as they become available. I know the people in the psych department, though, and I hope we can work out something for me to stay there, maybe doing the same things for a group of professors that I was doing for Dr. Melrose. Meanwhile, though, I'll have my hands full, trying to wrap up Dr. Melrose's grants, expenses, and research.

"Andy and I talked about it some last night. I know he won't be here on campus, but while he's in Liechtenstein, he might be able to co-ordinate the wrap-up of those projects with my help. At least then the already half-completed research won't have been a complete waste."

She went on, "We'd make a good team. As you may know, I graduated from Jericho State with honors in psychology, and I've worked in the field ever since then. I even co-authored some papers with Dr. Melrose, which, let's be honest, means I wrote them for him..."

Dr. Kopfmann jumped in at that point, "As I'm sure you surmised from your interviews last night, Dr. Melrose and I didn't agree on the interpretations of my research, and I'm sure that if I do take over his current research projects, I'll be nudging them in a somewhat different direction. Phillipa and I have agreed to continue to explore the possibilities today, though, to see what we can work out."

He looked at Phillipa and smiled. She smiled back at him and nodded.

"Meanwhile, can we explore these differences you had with Dr. Melrose a bit more?" asked Sergeant Scheffler.

174

"Certainly. As he announced when he introduced me. ... Oh, that's right. You weren't there for that. Well, anyway, when I was working with the Bunu gangs in both Vancouver and Vietnam, I discovered that primal scream therapy was a very effective way of identifying and understanding the group dynamics. Dr. Melrose really wasn't interested in that aspect of my work, but I was able to link his basic expositions of Freudian therapy with Dr. Arthur Janov's work on primal scream therapy. It turns out that the differences in how people scream in groups reflect a great deal about the dynamics of the group as well as about the individuals themselves. Dr. Melrose consistently ignored the primal scream portion of my research and that was something I had begun using effectively in my own clinical therapeutic interventions. All he ever talked about were the portions of my work that were classically Freudian. My work was much farther developed than that, and, I must confess, I was deeply upset by his refusal to recognize and acknowledge the differences... along with the intellectual growth I went through myself as I put the two strategies together. I think his refusal to recognize and acknowledge my developments in this area had a ... well, a noticeable impact on my career. He kept making my work look like 'here's yet another Melrose student rehashing Melrose's work', but mine was different. It was unique, and it deserved better than that. He should have been encouraging more recognition for me instead of trying to force my work into his mold so that he could take all the glory for himself."

Andy took a deep breath. "Instead of my riding his coattails, which was how he portrayed our relationship, he was beginning to try to ride on my

175

slowly building reputation. It was as if he was saying to the profession, 'Hey, this guy is good and he was my student, so I deserve most of the credit for his success.' It really wasn't fair. He was trying to keep me down while I was still working my way up, and he was trying to steal the credit for my success.

"He tried to buy me off, in a way, by recommending me for my current well-paid study leave in Liechtenstein and by paying for my trip back here for this conference. Don't get me wrong – I was grateful for those things. Also, he was very accommodating while I took a year off from grad school to get my research back on track. I worked in restaurants in Vancouver then to support myself, but he ... and Phillipa... helped out a great deal with travel funds and grant applications so I could travel between Vietnam and Vancouver to complete my field research."

Sergeant Scheffler was surprised by Andy's lengthy response. He began to wonder, "Is that all? What's he trying to cover up? Is he being defensive?"

"Were you upset with him enough that you wanted to kill him?"

"Of course not. I was upset, but I still got a lot of value out of knowing him. I certainly had no reason to kill him."

☿♀

176

Chapter 22 – **Ruthie, Again**

Detective Newhouse's call at nine o'clock that morning woke Ruthie up. She rolled over and picked up her cell phone from its charging base.

"Hello?" she groaned in a sleepy voice.

She hoped it wasn't Roddie Castman. 'I wore him out last night,' she thought to herself. 'There's no way he'll be awake yet.' And then she remembered that it couldn't be Roddie because she'd given him the number of the women's abuse center when he asked for her phone number.

"Dr. Westover, this is Detective Newhouse from the Jericho Police Department. We talked last night at the Hilton."

"Yes?"

"I have a few more questions I need to ask you. I'll be there in half an hour."

Ruthie couldn't believe the detective didn't ask if it would be convenient.

"What?" she asked incredulously.

"I have a few more questions I need to ask, and they can't wait any longer. I'll be there in half an hour. If you have classes or clients to see this morning, you may have to cancel or reschedule them. If it'll help, I don't think I'll be more than an hour."

"Can't we do it now, on the phone."

"No, I'll be there in thirty minutes."

In the half hour that elapsed, Ruthie took a quick shower, dried her hair, put on minimal makeup, got dressed and started some coffee. Ruthie was so presentable when Detective Newhouse arrived that the detective thought, "Well, I guess she made it home early last night after all."

Ruthie welcomed her politely and offered her some coffee. But she didn't ask, "Would you like some coffee?" Instead, she asked, "How do you take your coffee?" guessing correctly that Detective Newhouse would want, maybe even feel the need for, some coffee that morning.

Detective Newhouse tried to take it all in stride. "Regular is good for me."

"Regular?" asked Ruthie. "I never know for sure what that means. For some people 'regular' means 'black' and for others it means 'one sugar, one cream'. I've even met some people who think it means 'double-double'. Which is it for you?"

Detective Newhouse had never heard *anyone* use 'regular' to mean 'black' or 'double-double'. She assumed Ruthie was trying to one-up her.

"Oh, anything is fine. You choose."

Ruthie was caught off-guard by that response. She expected to be in control of the interview, and Detective Newhouse had very subtly taken away the control by not answering her question but by making Ruthie make the coffee decision. It was trivial game-playing between the two of them, with each of them trying to keep the other one off balance.

While Ruthie was pouring the coffee, she thought, "Black. I'll give it to her black, and we'll *see* if she cares."

Detective Newhouse opened the interview by asking Ruthie about her childhood.

Ruthie looked at her with what Detective Newhouse took to be a challenging expression.

"My mother was a stripper and hooker. My father sold used cars. When I was in high school, I decided I didn't want to end up like them, so I stopped partying and buckled down. I'm glad I did. I have just what I wanted but it's something they never really got: a steady job with lots of freedom to do whatever and *whom*ever I want. It's very freeing."

That brief autobiography often left people shocked into silence, but Detective Newhouse had been on the streets herself, both as a teenager and later as a police officer. She had talked with lots of women with Ruthie's background. The only difference was that Ruthie, like Detective Newhouse, had straightened herself around. But had she?

"Tell me about your therapy sessions."

Ruthie wasn't about to volunteer anything. "Okay, what do you want to know?"

"Well, you're a sex therapist, right?"

"Yes..."

"What kinds of issues do you deal with?

"I treat whatever sexual issues the clients present with," replied Ruthie.

"What are some of the more common issues?"

They continued their banter back and forth and finally, Ruthie asked, "What does all this have to do with last night?"

"You told several people that you expected fireworks last night. You were going to challenge some of Dr. Melrose's findings?"

"You bet I was. He was so wrapped up in the classical Freudian tradition that he couldn't see that there are other sides of the human sexual relationship."

"Such as?"

"Well, a lot of people who have sex issues were abused physically or sexually when they were children. This is an important and well-known phenomenon, and Dr. Melrose was well aware of it, but Freud pretty much ignored it."

"So you treated the victims of sexual abuse." Detective Newhouse stated it as a fact but was really asking a question, a questioning technique that both she and Lieutenant Randall used.

"In a sense, yes, but only to the extent that it affected their sex lives in the present. We have to delve into their pasts some, of course, to get at what is bothering them, but my approach is very much based on dealing with the present, how people feel and how they act – how they cope with the present. That's what's important – dealing with whatever the present has to offer. Dr. Melrose spent all his time doing Freudian analysis, even though he wasn't formally and legitimately trained to do it. He used his techniques to seduce his patients; I use my techniques to help them, to open them up, to get them past the hurdles they have to deal with, whether they were sexually abused as children or just raised by uptight prudes."

"Wait a minute! Dr. Melrose seduced his patients?"

"Sure he did. Everyone knows that."

"How do *you* know he did?"

"He told me one night when we were lying in bed together. He said … well, let's leave it that he bragged about it to me during a somewhat intimate and careless moment."

Detective Newhouse didn't flinch, but she did register that Ruthie seemed quite open about having had a sexual relationship with Dr. Melrose.

"Did that concern you?"

"Of course it did. He hired me, and I hoped to use his reputation as a steppingstone to bigger and better things. I couldn't very well do that if the old lecher lost his license and maybe even lost his job here at Jericho State, could I?"

"What was your own beef with him?"

"I didn't have any so-called 'beef' with him. The source of potential conflict between us was that I had moved on, beyond his research. I was moving away from kow-towing to everything he said. I was determined not to be a rubber stamp for his pet theories."

"Did that cause you any problems professionally?"

"None. We disagreed, but we maintained a good academic relationship."

That wasn't what Detective Newhouse had heard. She pressed on.

"And yet he was blocking your promotion to full professor and would likely stand in your way for other academic honors."

Again it was a statement. Detective Newhouse had developed a way a making aggressive, challenging statements that were really questions. It was a technique she learned as a teenager when she, herself, was surviving on the streets.

"That wasn't anything. I realized I'd have to cozy up to him a bit more, but he was easily persuadable, if you know what I mean..."

"But you resented having to use sex to get what you had earned as a researcher. You didn't think it was fair to have to use sex to get something you deserved anyway."

"What are you," asked Ruthie, "a prosecutor or something?"

"I'm just asking..." Trudy let it hang and softened her tone. "It wasn't fair, was it."

"Fair, schmair. I had no problem using sex to get what I wanted. I learned that at an early age."

"Nevertheless, his blocking your promotion must have upset you."

"Yes, it did. But not enough to kill him."

"With Dr. Melrose dead, the promotion will go much more easily now, won't it? Wasn't he the primary person who was standing in the way of your promotion and maybe even in the way of that thing you wanted... a chair or whatever it's called?"

"An endowed chair. With it, I wouldn't have to teach as much, and I could spend more time developing my research and therapeutic protocols."

"But Dr. Melrose stood in the way of your getting that?"

"I assumed he did. He *was* becoming more demanding after hours."

"And you resented that."

"You betcher sweet bippie I did."

Detective Newhouse filed that response and continued, "Let's go over what happened after Dr. Melrose left the room."

"I did that last night."

"I know, but maybe something will occur to you now, this morning, that didn't last night. This is pretty standard routine for us to ask people to go over things the next day. Let's start with the few minutes leading up to when Dr. Melrose left the room. Did you notice anything unusual about his speech or movements then?"

"I thought we all told you. His speech got a bit slower – just a bit, it wasn't a big change. It was like he was working hard to say the words correctly. And I noticed he slurred a couple of words, something that was uncommon for him."

"Anything else?"

"Well, he might have stumbled a bit. I saw him reach out and touch Phillipa's elbow one time. I didn't know whether he was signaling her something, trying to get her attention, or maybe just regaining his balance... I don't know..."

"Okay after he left the room, what happened with you?"

"I was just standing there, and I could see Andy and Robin and Roddie all looking in my direction. I was fed up with them and fed up with having to hold them off, and so I left the room. I'm not sure if I announced it, but I think I told someone I was going to using the ladies' restroom."

"Now think carefully. Where did you go?"

Ruthie began using measured tones as she closed her eyes to visualize her movements.

"The restrooms were straight ahead in the hallway, so to throw people off, I turned left outside the room. I hurried down that corridor until I reached a stairwell. I looked back to make sure no one was following me, and I quickly dodged through that door and went up to the third floor. "From there I took the elevator down to the basement. I don't remember exactly which way I went after I got down there. I was wandering a bit, looking for a way to get out to the alleyway when I met this really cute young guy, a sous chef who was going into the kitchen. I asked him how I could get out of the hotel some back way. He said, 'Come with me,' and I said, 'Anytime.'"

Again, Ruthie smiled a smile that said, "See, I can conquer men anytime I want to..."

"He took me through the kitchen into a lower loading dock area. We sat there and shared a smoke. He wanted my name and number, but I wouldn't give them to him. I got his, though. You want them? He's *very* cute." Ruthie smiled as if she was giving Detective Newhouse her castoffs.

"Yes, I'd better have his name and number in case we need to follow up with him." Detective Newhouse was exasperated but tried not to show it. Was everything about sex and seduction with Ruthie?

Ruthie got up and found his name and number. Then she continued, "I got him to show me to the main elevator bank, took the elevator up to the second floor, went back to the conference room, and that's when I saw James on the floor with people gathered around him."

Detective Newhouse made a mental note to see if there were videos of the basement level, kitchen, and alleyway to confirm Ruthie's account of where she had been and when and with whom.

She thought to herself, "Most people still don't seem to realize that Big Brother really is watching you. There's so much security video around these days, we can usually check on your movements almost anywhere you go."

What she said to Ruthie, though, was, "Mmmm. This is good coffee! What kind is it?"

"It's Kona coffee, medium roast. I order it directly from Hawaii. I'm glad you like it."

She picked up the bag. "Here, take the rest of this bag with you. I have more in the cupboard. I order it by the case."

"Thanks!"

In truth, Detective Newhouse really did like the coffee, which surprised her, because she rarely liked coffee black. But in her little power struggle with Ruthie, she wasn't going to admit that she didn't take her coffee black... and she was glad she had tried it that way with that brand."

They spent the next ten minutes reviewing what happened between the time Ruthie returned to the room and when the police arrived.

At the end of that time, Ruthie looked at her watch rather obviously, which irritated Detective Newhouse enough that she asked a few more questions even though she was about finished.

"After we let you go last night, what happened?"

"Is this relevant to your investigation?"

"We won't know until you answer."

"Okay. I suggested to Dwayne Carter that we go for a drink, but he said he had too much work to do and he was hoping you folks will let him go back to New Haven sometime this morning."

"Did he say anything more about Dr. Melrose or what might have happened in the room?"

"Hmmm, not that I recall. It was a brief conversation."

"And then?"

"I made the mistake of going to the elevator right then without looking to see who else was waiting. Robin Bobbitt and Roddie Castman were both there, and Roddie suggested the three of us go for a drink. I thought, 'Oh well, here we go. I'll give this yokel a night to remember.' Robin declined the invitation, and Roddie took me down to the bar, where we had a few drinks. I left his room and a *very* exhausted man at about four o'clock this morning. He was what I call 'orgasmically comatose.' "

"Did he say anything about Dr. Melrose while you were together?"

"I don't think he was thinking about James..."

"Nothing? Not even during the drinks?"

"Oh sure, he said stuff like, 'Wow, I wonder what happened', and 'What was he like?'"

She bit her lip. She wished she hadn't said that because she knew what was coming next.

"What did you tell him?"

"I said, 'He's a tired old man who can't face the fact that he hasn't kept up with our field. He continues to roar like an old lion that's been expelled from the pride, but people don't pay much attention to him anymore.'"

"Will you miss him?"

The question caught Ruthie off guard again, and Ruthie could see that Detective Newhouse enjoyed one-upping her repeatedly.

She thought for moment, sipped her coffee, and said, "Not much. He wasn't great in bed, but it was fun arousing the old geezer now and then. And as you've mentioned several times, he was impeding my academic progress. I will say this, though: he was a big help early in my career."

"How's that?"

"He recommended me for this job, and he urged the department to grant me early promotion and tenure. Those things made my life much easier. The problem was that he thought I owed him forever for what he had done for me, and not just sexually but academically, too. He even had me cover some of his classes whenever he couldn't make it, but he never offered to cover any of mine."

☿

Chapter 23 – **Back at the Hotel**

Sergeant Houston notified all the taxicab, limo, and van services, telling them to let her know if Dr. Kopfmann or Phillipa tried to book a trip anywhere out of town. Then she sent a notice to the airlines that they were not to let either of them board a plane going anywhere, but especially not to Germany, Switzerland, France, Belgium, Canada, or Vietnam, ... anywhere out of the country, actually ... without first checking with the Jericho Police.

Then she went to the Jericho Hilton to visit Dr. Carter and Roddie Castman.

" 'R' before 'S'," she joked to herself, noting the third letters of their last names, and she called Dr. Carter on the hotel house phone.

"Dr. Carter, this is Sergeant Houston of the Jericho Police. I have just a few more points I need to ask you about. I'll be up to your room in just a couple of minutes."

When she arrived, Dr. Carter had his suitcase packed and had some papers on the desk, next to his briefcase.

"I hope this won't take long," he said, "but I'll do whatever I can to co-operate. What do you want to know?"

He gestured for Sergeant Houston to take the easy chair in the room while he turned his desk chair to face her.

"Had you ever met Dr. Melrose before last night?"

"Sure. Several times at conferences. Never anywhere else. We never invited him to give presentations at Yale, and he never invited me to give any seminars here at Jericho State.

"At conferences, we introduced ourselves to each other, and we often chatted at various cocktail parties sponsored by book publishers or others flogging their wares. I think the longest we ever actually spoke together was maybe five or ten minutes."

"Did you clash or disagree about much?"

"Not in person. We maintained a polite manner between us."

" 'Not in person.' Does that mean you clashed otherwise?"

"In print we had some minor disagreements. He was pure Freudian, but I was a dream analyst. I used other frameworks for analysis in addition to Freud. The disagreements were minor, as I said. I never felt as if there was anything major at stake. We tended to agree about most things most of the time."

"Of the people in the room last night, were there any with whom Dr. Melrose had major disagreements?"

"None that I knew of. I don't really know these people very well. I tend to stay on the East Coast for conferences; I came to this one only because I was invited to be on different panel yesterday morning, and I stayed because I was aware of the work by Kopfmann and Westover, and wanted to see how they and Melrose might deal with their differences."

Sergeant Houston asked herself, "Did he just volunteer too much? If he did, why?"

Dr. Carter answered that question as he continued.

"Sergeant, as I explained last night, I would really like to leave as soon as possible so I can get back to New Haven for my afternoon seminar. Is there a chance I can leave now?"

She thought to herself, "I'm thinking he's spilling everything now so he can leave quickly," and she texted Lieutenant Randall, "My guess is Carter is out of it. Okay to let him go?"

Lieutenant Randall texted back immediately, "If you think so."

Sergeant Houston smiled. He was avoiding the responsibility himself, but more importantly he was trusting her judgement, and that pleased her.

"I see you're packed. You may go, but we may have to call you or invite you back if there's anything that comes up that we haven't anticipated."

Dr. Carter threw the papers into his briefcase and thanked Sergeant Houston as he picked up his suitcase. He ushered her out of the room and hurried to the elevator. He hoped to make good time to Midway Airport, drop his rental car quickly and catch a flight to New Haven. He had a chance if there were no further delays.

As they rode down the elevator together, Dr. Carter gave her his card and said, "Call me if you need me. I'll call the hotel to check out while I'm on the road ... don't worry, it'll be hands-free with Siri ...   and I'll call the airline. I think I can make an early afternoon flight."

As he rushed to the carpark, Sergeant Houston went to the house phones to call Roddie Castman.

- - -

"Hello?" Roddie sounded groggy.

"Hello, Dr. Castman, this is Sergeant Houston of the Jericho Police. We have a few more questions I need to ask you. I'll be up to your room in a few minutes."

Roddie wasn't a doctor. He hadn't finished his doctoral dissertation at The University of Minnesota and was what educators referred to as an ABD – All-But-Dissertation, meaning he had finished all his coursework and qualifying exams for the PhD but he hadn't finished his dissertation. As a result, he bounced around from school to school, hoping to be taken on somewhere eventually as a full-time, permanent lecturer.

"Wait..." he said as he slowly woke up. "Your call woke me. I can't see anyone now. Given me time to shower, brush my teeth, and get dressed, okay?"

"Twenty minutes," said Sergeant Houston, and she took the elevator up to his room where she parked outside his door. She had read about a few cases where people asked for some time get showered and dressed when they already were, and they snuck out while no one was watching them. Sergeant Houston wasn't going to let that happen with Roddie.

Exactly twenty minutes later, Sergeant Houston knocked on Roddie Castman's door. When he finally opened the door, his hair was wet, the bed was a mess, and things were strewn all over the room. Sergeant Houston took one look and said, "Let's go down to the lobby for this."

Roddie had nothing new to tell her, though, other than that he'd had the experience of his life with Ruthie after they went to his room. "That woman is an ex-pert!" he enthused. "I sure hope I can hook up with her just one more time before I die..."

"Why did you come to this conference?"

"I'm on a year-to-year contract where I'm teaching now – the University of Wisconsin at Stephens Point," he said. "I need to keep attending conferences, and I need to keep talking with places that might have visiting positions for next year. Doing this keeps me supported, and eventually I'll find a more permanent situation I hope."

"But why *this* conference? Aren't there more general conferences dealing with psychology where your job prospects would be better?"

"Yeah, you're right, I've never scored a job at an ASP meeting, but when people talk about sex they get more interested. I've never **not** scored that way at an ASP meeting."

"You're wearing a wedding ring."

"Yeah, well, what she don't know..."

"Did you talk with Dr. Melrose at all before he died?"

"Nope. In fact, I'd never heard of the man before last night, but that's not saying much. I pay attention to the women at these conferences, not the men. The women and the free food!"

"You'd never read anything by him or met him before?"

"Not that I can recall."

Sergeant Houston believed him, but she also didn't care for his tone and attitude. So she didn't bother to tell him he could leave Jericho whenever he wanted to.

Chapter 24 – **Robin, Again**

At 8:30 that morning, Detective Steglitz phoned the home of Dr. Robin Bobbitt.

A woman's voice answered, "Dr. Bobbitt's residence."

"This is Detective Steglitz calling from the Jericho Police Department. May I please speak with Dr. Bobbitt?"

"I'm sorry, he's gone for the day."

"Can you tell me where he is now?"

"He ordinarily stops for coffee on his way to the studio. He'll either be at Starbucks, at the studio, or somewhere between the two."

Detective Steglitz called Dr. Bobbitt's cell phone, but it went to voice mail. Steglitz left a message and drove to the studio.

The studio for Dr. Bobbitt's "Round Pegs, Round Holes" programs was a modest brick building next to a plaza on the southwest edge of town. There was a small office with a receptionist just inside the door, and just beyond the office there was a large engineering studio that looked onto two recording areas. One of the recording rooms was a small radio studio with room for three people, each with their own headset and microphone. The other recording room was a full television production studio with cameras, lights, sets, and boom microphones.

Robin was putting the finishing touches on a session for radio when Detective Steglitz was admitted to the engineering studio. When the session was over, the detective insisted that he needed at least a half hour and maybe more to follow up with some questions. Robin's producer was there and tried to object, saying they were already behind schedule, but Detective Steglitz insisted.

"We have several leads that must be examined today," he said. "We will greatly appreciate Dr. Bobbitt's co-operation."

"I told you everything I know last night," said Robin.

Detective Steglitz gave the standard reply: "I know, but we find that when we go over things again a day later, people remember things or say things a bit differently in ways that can sometimes be helpful.

"Let's begin with what happened after you left last night."

"I went to the elevator and that geeky guy from Wisconsin with the bright plaid sportcoat and the bow tie tagged along. While we were waiting for the elevator, Ruthie joined us. Mr. Bow Tie suggested we all go for a drink to unwind after everything we'd been through. I didn't care for him, and I had been snubbed by Ruthie a couple of times that evening, so I begged off and went straight home.

"At home, I poured myself a three-ounce shot of Ledaig scotch on the rocks and went to bed when I finished it. My alarm woke me at eight o'clock this morning, I got up, showered and dressed, stopped for coffee on the way here, and when I got here, we recorded a portion of an upcoming program."

"The man with the bow tie was Mr. Castman. What did he and you talk about?"

"He wanted to know how I got into what he termed, 'the media therapy business', and did I need an assistant. He actually gave me his résumé. I tried to be polite, but he was very pushy. To tell the truth, I was relieved when Ruthie came along and he redirected his attention toward her. I'll bet a Starbucks dark chocolate macchiato they spent the night together. Ruthie loves torturing and introducing goofy innocents to her techniques. He was a perfect mark for her."

"What do you know about her relationship with Dr. Melrose?"

"He had some sort of power over her. Maybe it was just his position in the department and as a once-respected dean of the profession. Whatever it was, she felt obliged to humor him now and then. They clashed at times, too, but she always tried to smooth it over. Maybe it was just that she was trying to use him professionally... that's how it seemed, but I always wondered if there was more. Maybe she had some sort of Electra-like devotion to a father figure? I don't know.

"It always bothered me when she and I were together back when I was a graduate student. We were half living together, but I knew she was still sleeping with James now and then. I wrote it off as her way of trying to get ahead in her career, but I didn't like it. Judging from the way she was cozying up to him at dinner last night, I'm guessing it was still going on. That annoyed me, but more about her than about him."

"So, you were jealous of Dr. Melrose?"

"In a way, I guess I was. I had been deeply attached to Ruthie when I was in grad school. I thought we had developed an ongoing relationship. But she dropped me the minute I finished my last exam. 'It was good while it lasted, Robbie,' she told me, 'but now it's time for both of us to move on.'"

"But you said last night that you hoped to hook up with her again at least for the night..."

"You know how sometimes you want to prove something? You're angry when a relationship ends, and you want to extract something from the other person? That feeling lasts, you know."

That response gave Detective Steglitz pause. It fit right in with Robin's desire for revenge against Dr. Melrose for not paying the referral fees. He thought to himself, "This guy has a pretty nasty temperament under it all. He does stuff for revenge. He just raised himself on the suspicion list."

"Okay, let's go over what happened at dinner."

"As I said last night, Ruthie was on the right of James, Andy was on her right, and Phillipa was on Andy's right. I was on the left of James, between him and Phillipa. Ruthie was playing up to James big time, and Andy was trying to get Ruthie to pay attention to him. Phillipa would rather have spent time talking with Andy, but since she and I were pretty much being ignored by everyone else, we chatted together now and then whenever Ruthie and James weren't holding forth."

The tone of his response made him seem quite bitter. Detective Steglitz thought, "How does this guy do so well on television when he has so much bitterness?"

"Did you resent Dr. Melrose for being in control of the conversation?"

"In a way, of course. I'm used to being in charge these days, but the adjustment was easy. This was a night to honor James. I could swallow my pride for that. After all, I owed that man a lot. He got me into graduate school despite my spotty background, and he kept me in when I was struggling.

"And since you'll want to ask about it, yes I was upset about his not paying the referral fees. I thought we had an agreement; we shook hands on it. In fact, because he had helped me so much in graduate school, I even cut him a deal compared with the referral fees I get from other therapists even though he didn't need the money any more than I did. I can't understand why he would cheat me like that. And actually, I did need that money because I wanted to expand our syndication network; we needed the referral fees to help fund it up front until the additional ad revenue came in."

And then Robin asked, "Is there any word, yet, on the cause of death? I'm still hoping he died of natural causes and we can forget about all this stuff. I'm sure it hasn't been easy for any of the people who were there."

That was the softer, caring side of Robin that Detective Steglitz had seen on TV.

"We still don't have any confirmed cause of death," was all he would say about it. "We'll know more later today or tomorrow."

Detective Steglitz shifted gears again. "How upset do you think the others were with Dr. Melrose?"

"Well, to cut to the chase, I don't think any of them was upset enough to kill him. But I also think that there must have been a dozen or more people in that room who didn't like James for one reason or another."

"Let's begin with Dr. Kopfmann. What was his grudge, as you saw it?"

"I don't know that he had much of a legitimate complaint. I know he thought James was misrepresenting his work, but he was doing what he could to counteract that. Meanwhile James had provided him with generous support, both financially and academically. I think Andy was also upset because Ruthie was playing up to James, and he had hopes of spending the night with her last night. He really couldn't control his drooling over her – figuratively, I mean. And once it was clear James was dead, Andy very clearly thought that would open the door for him with Ruthie. But he's good-looking enough and a good enough conversationalist, I'm sure he could have found a substitute. He didn't need to kill James just to get a shot at having a night with Ruthie. There were other fish in the sea there last night."

"What about Dr. Westover? What was her gripe about Dr. Melrose?"

"I think her main problem was that he was blocking the promotion she wanted. In my opinion, he was right, and she was premature in pushing for a promotion, especially for an endowed chair, but she sure seemed to think she should get there, and from what I heard, he was a major opponent of giving her the promotion. I can't believe the old goat still had some academic integrity, but I guess he did.

"She tried to cozy up to him, she tried to reference his work positively, she slept with him, she tantalized him, but none of that was working any longer. I'm sure she was getting frustrated by her inability to sway him the way she had swayed everyone else and by not having the power over him that she'd had in the past. There's no doubt, now, that with him out of the way, her path to that endowed chair will be much smoother. I just hope she has the good sense not to push for it too soon – it would look really inappropriate if she started pushing for the promotion right after James died."

Just as Detective Steglitz was wrapping up the interview, Lieutenant Randall sent a text to all those who were out doing interviews that morning.

When you're done, come to the office. It was murder. Don't rush, but don't stop for donuts on the way.

Detective Steglitz was slightly amused by Lieutenant Randall's reference to donuts. Everyone in the homicide division knew that Mike Randall didn't fit the image of being a donut-loving cop. To make his point, he banned donuts from his office. He was so strongly opinionated about donuts that one day three months ago, his team got together and brought in vegetables and dip hidden in donut boxes, much to the amusement of everyone on the force.

♂♀

Interlude:
Lieutenant Randall has the evidence now and is about to solve the crime. There have been some hints along the way, and you have probably picked up on those hints, but there hasn't been any really solid evidence yet. Using those hints, can you guess who the murderer was, how it was done, and what the motive was?

Chapter 25 -- **Reports**

With his team expectantly gathered around the scarred table in the meeting room at police headquarters, Lieutenant Randall said, "First the videos. Officers Keene and Miller spent the past hour going over all the security videos from the hotel. They saw absolutely nothing to contradict what anyone told us last night. Dr. Melrose went to the men's room, and he did stumble a bit as he went in. Nobody followed him in there, and nobody else went in until after he left. When he came out about ten minutes later, he was stumbling, and he had that gash and bruise on his forehead. He didn't encounter anyone on his way back to the room, and about a half minute or so after Dr. Melrose fell into the conference room, Dr. Kopfmann approached the men's room from the side of the elevators and went in. He came out about ten seconds later and went right to the conference room himself.

"Dr. Bobbitt did indeed wander the halls on the other side of the hotel with his cell phone to his ear the entire time, and Dr. Westover did go into the stairwell, emerge on the third floor, and take the elevator to the basement. The next we saw her was out on the loading dock because there are no security cameras in the basement or in the kitchen. She was there for just a few minutes, as she said, sharing a joint with someone from the kitchen staff. ... well, sharing what looked like a hand-rolled cigarette and was probably a joint.

"After we finished with them last night, Dr. Kopfmann left with Ms. MaGraw, and Drs. Bobbitt and Westover met Castman at the elevator. Dr. Bobbitt left for the evening, but Dr. Westover and Dr. Castman had some drinks in the bar before, apparently retiring to his room. We didn't pick up what time she left, but she was at home for Det. Newhouse to interview at 9:30 this morning. So, it pretty much unfolded the way everyone said.

"Let's turn to the Butt Report, now."

Patrolmen Keene and Miller exchanged glances as they stifled chuckles.

"There was no indication that Dr. Melrose died of any conceivable natural cause – stroke, heart attack, diabetic coma, cancer, infection, nothing. Dr. Butts did, however, think there was something odd-smelling about his stomach contents, and so she sent them out for analysis. She also took blood samples and asked for a full tox screen. Bless her for pushing to get the results quickly because some of these possible suspects are leaving town, and we need to stop them, if necessary."

Sergeants Scheffler and Houston were used to Lieutenant Randall's technique of dribbling out the information, but they were still on edge, along with Detectives Newhouse and Steglitz, eager to hear what he really wanted to say. "Stop them, if necessary?" thought Sergeant Scheffler. "You must know who we have to stop. Why drag it out?"

"Well, the stomach contents were pretty much as expected: salad, steak, potatoes, and coffee. No wine or alcohol."

"So what was the smell?" asked Detective Newhouse. She hadn't learned, yet, not to push Lieutenant Randall when he was presenting the evidence.

"Dr. Butts wasn't sure about the smell. It was just that something didn't seem right, and so she sent a sample to the lab, and they couldn't find any food that might have gone bad. ..."

Detective Newhouse pushed herself back a few inches from the table and crossed her legs in exasperation.

"They did say there was something there, though, that took a couple of hours for them to figure out. It seemed fish-based..."

This time nobody interrupted him and so he continued.

"That was all they could say right then. But the tox screen seemed to go along with that."

Everyone remained quiet. Detective Newhouse thought to herself, though, "Aha! Someone poisoned the salad dressing with a poison that would be confused with the taste of anchovies in the dressing!"

The lieutenant hesitated again.

"Dr. Melrose was definitely poisoned. The poison was something you may have heard of, but it's not easy to pronounce: it was tetrodotoxin."

Pause. Lieutenant Randall said it as if everyone should know what that was, even though he'd had to look it up himself.

Finally, Sergeant Houston asked, "Tetrodo-who?" and everyone quietly sighed in relief that she had asked.

"Its formal name is 'tetrodotoxin'" replied Lieutenant Randall, and he smiled. "I had to look it up myself. Here's what I found," and he read:

> Tetrodotoxin is a nonprotein aminohydroquinazoline compound with a heterocyclic structure. It is water-soluble and heat-resistant and does not alter the taste or appearance of the fish.

Everyone, including Lieutenant Randall, laughed as he struggled with the pronunciations.

Detective Newhouse said, "But he didn't eat any fish! How did that get into him?" She was still thinking about the salad dressing.

Sergeant Houston had a different idea, but she didn't say anything yet.

Lieutenant Randall dragged it out some more.

"Based on his stomach contents, it could have been added to the salad dressing..."

He paused and let that sink in, and Detective Newhouse quietly congratulated herself. ... until she realized from the way lieutenant was presenting the information, salad dressing was not the source of the poison.

Detective Newhouse was still on the offensive/defensive, though. "But no one saw anyone tamper with any of his food. Sure, something sort of fishy could have blended in with the anchovies in the salad dressing, but no one saw anything."

"You're right, Detective Newhouse. I doubt if it was put on his salad. Almost certainly, it was given to him after dinner."

"After dinner? Where?" asked Sergeant Scheffler. "Nobody reported anything that seemed suspicious. Did he get a snack or a drink somewhere that no one mentioned?"

"Not that I know of," answered Lieutenant Randall. "My bet is that it was given to him once he got into that room."

Sergeant Scheffler laughed. "Lieutenant, you never bet except on a sure thing. What are you holding back, huh?"

Lieutenant Randall smiled again.

"Well, let's look at the forensics reports. First, Dr. Melrose's coffee cup. Once Holly got the tox-screen report, he knew what to check for in the coffee, and sure enough, there was enough tetero-whatsit in that cup to kill several people. That's how the poison was administered. While he was wandering around the room, talking with all those different people, someone slipped it into his coffee. It was sitting there at the head table, and anyone could have strolled by and dropped the poison into his cup."

"How do you know that?" asked Detective Steglitz. "MaGraw could have put it into the coffee before she brought it into him. She wouldn't have been observed doing that if she poisoned it out wherever she got the coffee, and no one would have been the wiser."

Lieutenant Randall hesitated a moment. He hadn't thought about that possibility. But then he realized it couldn't have happened that way.

"Excellent point, Detective," he said. "Let me carry on, and I think I can answer it."

"Do we have good reports on who walked by or was near Dr. Melrose's coffee at the head table?" asked Patrolman Keene.

"The reports are far from perfect," Lieutenant Randall admitted, but we know that Ms. MaGraw was there next to him when he made the introductions, and we know that Drs. Westover, Kopfmann, Bobbitt, and Carter all spoke with him near there at various times."

"How long does ... that poison ... take to work, and how does it work?" asked Detective Steglitz.

"Here's what Bob Holly sent me in email[*]:

> Tetrodotoxin is a heat-stable, water-soluble, nonprotein toxin that is 50 times more potent than strychnine. It acts by binding to sodium channels and blocking axonal nerve transmission, and results in ascending paralysis and respiratory

[*] See https://www.sciencedirect.com/topics/pharmacology-toxicology-and-pharmaceutical-science/tetraodontidae

failure. In addition to pufferfish, porcupine fish, and ocean sunfish, tetrodotoxin has been found in other marine animals…

The onset of symptoms of pufferfish poisoning may occur within 10 minutes of ingestion of toxic fish or be delayed for ≥4 hours. Severe cases are usually associated with ingestion of large amounts of toxin and early onset of symptoms. Initial symptoms include perioral paresthesias and numbness, nausea, and dizziness. Later, there may be more generalized paraesthesia and numbness, dysarthria, ataxia, ascending paralysis, and a variety of other symptoms, such as headache, hypersalivation, diaphoresis, vomiting, abdominal pain, and diarrhea. In the most severe cases there is widespread paralysis, respiratory failure, bradycardia and other arrhythmias, and hypotension.

Lieutenant Randall looked up. "Apparently, death can occur pretty quickly with a heavy dose, but it could stretch over several hours with a smaller dose. Likely the poisoner used this poison, hoping that Dr. Melrose would feel the symptoms after the session and die during the night, but he or she used way too much, leading to the doctor's death within half an hour or so.

"Pufferfish," said Sergeant Houston. "I thought so," and she nodded to herself.

"But he didn't eat any pufferfish," said Detective Newhouse.

She still didn't follow where Sergeant Houston was going. The others were confused, too.

"No," replied Sergeant Houston. "The poison was extracted from the pufferfish. The person who did this knew what he was doing. This took some planning, I expect, because it would take time to get the poison into this form."

"But who among our leading suspects would have any idea how to do that?" asked Detective Newhouse.

"Kopfmann," replied Sergeant Houston.

"Good work, Sergeant," said Lieutenant Randall. "Tell us how you got there."

"Someone reported that he had asked Ms. MaGraw and Dr. Melrose to provide some fugu as one of the hors d'oeuvres last night. Fugu is a pufferfish and really needs carefully trained chefs to prepare it so that people who eat it aren't poisoned. Also, while he was on his year off, he worked in restaurants in Vancouver and visited Vietnam. He probably learned about the poison and how to extract it then. I'm guessing he found a source of fugu before he arrived here and did the job himself. Of course, if there actually *had* been fugu served with the hors d'oeuvres after the session, that would be the perfect out for him... who would have suspected him of poisoning Dr. Melrose's coffee then?"

Sergeant Houston added, "Dr. Melrose was stumbling a bit as he left the conference room and again as he went into the men's room. Undoubtedly, he just fell onto the wash basin, and that's how he cut his forehead and banged the edge of his mouth. It's a miracle he made it back to the conference room before he died."

"This is all surmise, though," said Detective Steglitz. "He may have had the knowledge, and he could have done it, but that doesn't really rule anyone else out, does it?"

"Good thinking," said Lieutenant Randall. "And that's where the rest of the forensics analysis comes into play. As you know, Keene and Miller set up Holly's people with the garbage from that room, and it didn't take them long. They came up with a little vial with traces of tetrodoxo-whatever in it. And best of all, there are some nice, clean fingerprints on it. Our guess is that they're Dr. Kopfmann's prints."

"Well, let's not let him get away!" said Sergeant Scheffler.

And then he paused. "I don't believe it. I interviewed him this morning. He seemed so calm. He'd finally caved in and spent the night with MaGraw, and she was positively beaming. She clearly has plans for the two of them..."

He stood up. "Let me go bring him in."

"Relax, Sergeant. We have two officers in unmarked cars on the scene. They won't be going anywhere."

Sergeant Scheffler sat down and ran his right hand through his hair.

"I still don't believe it. And I must say, I feel sorry for MaGraw. She had been after for him for years, finally got him, and now this... Poor woman."

Detective Steglitz stepped in, "Okay, so we have method and opportunity, and I guess a motive, but it seems pretty weak. We know Dr. Melrose was poisoned with textrodo-something, and we know that a source of ... that... could have been fugu, a pufferfish. And we know ... or really I guess we just suspect ... we have his fingerprints on a vial containing the poison. It's weak if he gets a good attorney."

Lieutenant Randall smiled again. He was loving his team. "Weak how?" he asked.

"Well, if no one saw him administer the poison to the coffee, there's no evidence he did it. His attorney will argue someone stole it from him or pick-pocketed it from him. His attorney will argue that the others had even stronger motives than he did and brought the poison themselves to shift the blame onto Kopfmann. His attorney will point out that when I interviewed him this morning, he seemed calm. Who knows, maybe MaGraw lied to me and they spent the night together the night before, and she stole the poison from him then? Do we have anything else?"

"We'll find it," answered Lieutenant Randall. "We'll interview chefs in Vancouver where he worked and find out he had an unusual curiosity about fugu poisoning, and we'll check with every fishmonger in Liechtenstein and even Chicago to find someone who sold him the fugu fish. He left a trail, and we'll find it."

- - -

An hour later, they all got messages:

They're leaving together, and they have suitcases.

Lieutenant Randall texted back:

> Stop them and bring them both in. No cuffs unless
> necessary.

When Andy and Phillipa were brought to the station, they were taken directly to the conference room where the homicide team had met an hour earlier.

Lieutenant Randall greeted them.

"Thank you for coming in to talk with us," he said. "I see you both have suitcases with you. I hope you weren't planning to leave town."

Andy replied, "Well, we thought that after that extra questioning this morning, you were through with us and it would be okay for us to leave. It is, isn't it?"

Phillipa added, "I'm due some vacation time, and I'll get some compassionate leave, and so I was planning to go back to Liechtenstein with Andy for a few weeks. I can take care of the most pressing things from there via e-mail and then look after the rest of Dr. Melrose's research and grants when I return."

"Well, you're going to have to put those plans on hold for awhile. Dr. Kopfmann, we are going to hold you for questioning for sure, and we strongly suspect you murdered Dr. Melrose."

"**NO!!!!**" Phillipa screamed and slammed the table three or four times. "He didn't do it! He couldn't have!"

"Sergeant Houston and Detective Newhouse, will you please take Ms. MaGraw to an interview room and question her in greater detail. Dr. Kopfmann, I'm going take you to a separate interview room where you and I can talk further."

Andy collapsed as Lieutenant Randall read him his rights. He knew he was entitled to a lawyer, but he also suspected they had or would find enough evidence to convict him. He wouldn't be granted bail, and so he just went along with them to the interview room.

After Lieutenant Randall turned on the recorder, Andy asked, "What do you have?"

Lieutenant Randall was circumspect but gave him the gist of everything. "The poison, the fish it comes from, your job history and travels, the vial with prints that are probably yours... that's enough to hold you for sure."

"The prints are mine," Andy confessed.

"Tell us how and when and why," said Lieutenant Randall.

"I should wait and speak with a lawyer first," Andy said, "but what's the use? You've got all you need, I'm sure."

Andy unloaded.

"Early on I developed a dislike for Dr. Melrose. Ruthie and I had a thing going one weekend and the next thing I knew she ditched me and spent the night with him. I was jealous and I resented it. But I wasn't going to jeopardize my doctoral studies or change schools because of it. Instead I used him all I could, and it worked. He got me extra travel grants and he went to bat for me when I was trying to find a new research plan. I resented him, but I was grateful, too, because he was able to help me out so much back then.

"You're right. It was while I was working in restaurants in Vancouver and while I was doing research in Vietnam that I learned how deadly tetrodotoxin from fugu can be. I had no goal in mind, but I thought to myself at one point, 'I might be able to use this someday.'

"I tried to get hold of some while I was working in the PufferHouse restaurant in North Vancouver, but I couldn't get it there."

"So where *did* you get it?"

"On my last trip to Vietnam two years ago. I got it then. I still don't know why I got it, but maybe in the back of my mind I was thinking about James. I really hated him."

"You took it to Liechtenstein with you?"

"Yes, I knew when I was going there that I had been invited to this conference, courtesy of Dr. Melrose. I thought I'd bring it along, just in case."

"Then we come to the question of 'why?' Why did you hate him so much that you would plan this in such detail?"

Andy looked straight at Lieutenant Randall.

"He was a condescending old coot who was essentially stealing my soul, and he knew it. Yes, he had been helpful to me when I was a graduate student, but even then he wanted me to lie about my research in Rwanda and just make up things that would fit into his own paradigm. I wouldn't do it, but I didn't want to confront him too much then because he was being so helpful at the same time. So, he slept with my girlfriend, he tried to get me to do slipshod work, and then when I essentially made it on my own, doing some pretty amazing work, he kept trying to claim the ideas as his or as having come from his work. I hated him.

"Even last night, when he was introducing us, he practically stole my presentation. He was a despicable, desperate old man. It was easy... when no one was looking, I dumped the fugu toxin into his coffee. But then when he died so quickly, I knew I had to get rid of the vial it was in, and your officers wouldn't let anyone leave the room, so I just put it in the garbage. If the hotel staff had been able to get the garbage out, you'd never have gotten the vial with my fingerprints on it. I should've wiped it. Oh well.

"But if we'd had fugu as an hors d'oeuvre, I'd have waited and given the poison to him later. Then it would have seemed as if the fugu was improperly prepared. Or if I'd put less in his coffee, it might have acted less quickly – I really didn't expect it to hit him so fast. He should have died later last night."

- - -

During her interview down the hall, Phillipa was frantic. She was crying and confessing and quite beside herself. Or, more correctly, she was trying to

217

confess. She had no idea what Andy had done, but she wanted to take the blame. In less than ten minutes, she confessed that she had no idea how Dr. Melrose died but that she was happy to take the blame if that would save Andy.

"I always felt an attachment to Andy," she told Sergeant Houston and Detective Newhouse. I was so happy he was coming to the conference, and I was so pleased when he came to stay with me last night. It was like a dream come true for me, like a honeymoon almost."

She broke down in sobs again. Her dreams were shattered.

The two interviewers looked at each other and recognized that Phillipa was in a state of trauma. She had lost her boss, her lover, her hopes, her dreams, everything in the past eighteen hours. She was going to need some help.

"Ms. MaGraw, you've had a series of shocks," consoled Sergeant Houston. "If I know what your workplace is like, you'll be welcomed back, and people will do whatever they can to ease you back into the stream of things– at least that's how it usually works – but you're going to need some help from someone who isn't part of your workplace. I hope you'll get some."

- - -

That evening, after their children were in bed, Mike Randall sat at the kitchen table with his wife. "You know, Lou, I don't think anyone will miss the guy. Nobody liked him, as far as I can tell. Kopfmann will

218

go to prison for it; his life and career are done. He'll be lucky to get sous-chef jobs when he's out.

But the person who was really hurt was Phillipa MaGraw. It's not that she loved the old man or anything, but she was attached to him. And then to find out that her dream lover, a man she had finally been able to spend the night with, had killed him ... well, that crushed her. Houston and Newhouse checked her into the psych ward at Jericho General for a few days, just for observation and counseling. This will be so hard for her to deal with. I've asked them to check in on her after a week and again a few times after that. She was so competent at her job but had such a poor self-image... It makes no sense.

"Are you glad you caught him?" Louise asked.

"Yes. He was deranged in some strange way. I guess it happens every day that people think about killing someone over a woman or over some professional slight, but it really is sick to actually go through with it."

The End

♂♀

219

About the Author:

John P. Palmer was born and raised in Muskegon, Michigan. By his own admission, he barely graduated from Carleton College (Northfield, Minnesota) in 1965 with a major in economics and minors in mathematics and religion.

From 1965 – 67, he was a student at The Chicago Theological Seminary, where he was active in the Civil Rights and Anti-Vietnam-War movements. While there, he realized he loved economics and wasn't at all cut out to be a church minister, and so he switched to graduate school in economics at Iowa State University (Ames, Iowa) where he received his PhD in economics in 1971. That same year he accepted a position in the Economics Department of The University of Western Ontario (London, Ontario). He retired from there forty years later, in 2011.

A self-described dilettante, he has been a prize-winning photographer, an orchestra conductor, a sportscaster, an award-winning actor, and now a novelist. **Shrink-Wrapped Murder** is his fourth novel.

John has three children, seven grandchildren, and two great-grandchildren. He lives with his wife in London, Ontario, where he is still active (Covid permitting) in theatre, music, and sportscasting. He also likes to play bridge, watch sports on television, go for walks, and write intermittently on his blog, *EclectEcon.net*.

He can be reached via email at EclectEcon@gmail.com or on Facebook, to which he claims to be hopelessly addicted.

Acknowledgments:

Both **Shrink-Wrapped Murder** and **Murder at the Office Christmas Party** began their lives as short mystery dinner theatre plays, available in the short book, **Three Murder Mysteries**. Because of the pandemic of 2020, the local mystery dinner theatre companies in London, Ontario, put their productions on hold, and the plays were never used. Rather than let them sit idly on my hard drive, I decided to try to turn the plays into mystery novels. My first attempt, **Murder at the Office Christmas Party** went reasonably well, and I was encouraged to write this one next. Along the way I received some valuable feedback, suggestions, and support from many people, including:

> Jack Allingham
> Dilan Goonetilleke
> John Henderson
> Thomas Hinds
> Charlene McNabb
> Paul Merrifield
> Jacob Palmer
> Matthew Palmer
> Brian Quast
> Dale Tassi
> Carolle Trembley
> Vivian Trembley

An Excerpt from

Murder at the Office Christmas Party

(The first novel in which Lieutenant Randall appears)

Chapter 1 – **Carpooling**

"Do you two drive to work together *every* day?"

Brent Howard was in the back seat of Elizabeth's car on the way to work with Elizabeth Hurd and David Dekker.

David hesitated before answering. He was often a bit slow to respond.

"Pretty much," he dragged out. "My apartment is just a few blocks from Elizabeth's. We began car-pooling a few days after she started working with us."

"Well, thanks for making this detour to pick me up. My car's in the shop for the next few days, and they wouldn't give me a loaner."

The three of them worked at Arttekko, a mid-sized company on the edge of town, mass-producing framed art prints for hotels, offices, chain stores, and large high-rise office buildings.

"It works out well," added Elizabeth. "Most of the time David just walks to my place, and I drive because my car is newer than his. Besides," she said proudly, "I have a parking spot closer to the office. David is kind enough to pay for a lot of the gas, though."

And she smiled at David.

Brent wondered about the two of them. David was easily ten to fifteen years older than Elizabeth, and he seemed awfully bland to be spending so much time with a sharp executive-type woman like Elizabeth. ... and yet, they seemed to be together a lot of the time. They even had matching travel mugs for their coffee.

Elizabeth glanced at Brent and said, "Brent, we're happy to give a ride to work today, but can you find your own way to the Arttekko Christmas Party tonight? David and I have a bunch of things we have to take to the party, and we want to get there early to get set up."

"Of course. I'm sure someone else can take me. If not, I can just Uber it."

When they got to the office, Brent headed for the production area where he was the shop foreman, Elizabeth went to her office up on the second floor, and David went straight to the mailroom on the main floor.

As she was going up the stairs, Elizabeth had to lean hard against the handrail to avoid being brushed, "accidentally" of course, by Sean Jones, who also had an office upstairs. Their offices were on opposite sides of CEO Linda Batchly's corner office.

"Hey, Betsy! How's it going?" said Sean; as usual he was overly jovial in his morning greeting.

Elizabeth hated being called 'Betsy', and Sean knew it. He only did it to provoke her. Sean headed up Arttekko's production department, and Elizabeth ran the marketing department. It often seemed as if they were in competition with each other even though they had separate and distinct responsibilities within the company.

"You going to the company Christmas party tonight?" Sean asked.

"I wasn't going to go," she glared at him, "but David offered to drive us there and back, so I think I will."

She knew she was lying, and she expected that Sean knew she was lying. David had organized the party almost single-handedly, and there was no way she was going to miss it.

Sean continued down the stairs but muttered loudly, "What does she see in that dullard?"

As she reached the second floor, Elizabeth tried to put Sean Jones out of her mind and cheerfully said, "Good morning, May!"

May Chandler was Arttekko's telephone receptionist and secretary for the executives. Her desk was in an open foyer and office area at the top of the stairs

"How are you this morning?" Elizabeth asked.

May smiled. She liked Elizabeth and had enjoyed following her success at Arttekko.

"I'm *o-kay*," replied May with enthusiasm and a sparkle in her eyes. "Bill and I went to dinner and a movie last night while the kids were with his parents. It sure was nice, just the two of us!"

As Elizabeth was going into her office, May called out, "She wants to see you when you get a chance."

Elizabeth sighed. Working for Linda Batchly wasn't easy, but it had its advantages. The pay was good, and she was doing things she liked. Even better, she enjoyed *most* of the people she worked with.

Linda Batchly was a different kind of beast, though.

Elizabeth took off her trench coat and hung it on the hook behind her door. After turning on her computer, she took her binder of forecasts and market projections from the shelf and knelt on the chair-stool at her ergonomic desk … the kind that forced her to sit or kneel upright or allowed her to stand at her variable-height desk while she was working.

She quickly scanned her e-mail inbox. Not seeing anything that couldn't wait, she took her binder with her and tapped on the door to Ms. Batchly's office.

Linda Batchly was a tough, dynamic widow in her early fifties. Most people at Arttekko knew that she had become the driving force in the company long before her husband, Murray Batchly, had his heart attack. She was the reason the firm had morphed into a world-class competitor in its industry.

"Come," said Linda to the door. Just the one word; nothing else.

Elizabeth opened the door and took a step inside, but only one step. It wasn't a tentative step; it was just that she knew you had to wait to be invited before you went any farther into Linda's office or before you sat down there.

Linda didn't issue an invitation, so Elizabeth just stood there, inside the door, waiting for her to say something.

After what was probably only ten seconds but felt like two minutes, Elizabeth spoke.

"You wanted to see me?"

"You missed with your forecasts by ten percent last month," said Linda. "What happened?"

"I wondered that myself," Elizabeth replied, "and so I've been looking at industry-wide forecasts. It turns out the entire industry was off the mark by over fifteen percent, so we did pretty well in comparison…"

"It's not good enough," interrupted Linda. "Forecasts that far off cost us money. Last month we had to put a bunch of these yahoos on overtime and have them come in on weekends as well just to fill the orders. What happened? How could you be so far off?"

Elizabeth was prepared for this, but she hadn't expected to be hit with it so hard so early in the morning, especially on the day of the Arttekko Christmas party, as if that mattered to Linda Batchly.

"Remember that huge order we had from Drom Hotels? You said not to schedule the production until we got a fifty-percent deposit from them, given their track record. Then when we got their deposit, they had a clause in the contract that said they'd pay us less if we didn't deliver all the artwork before the end of the month. When you and Sean and I discussed it, we agreed that the necessary overtime would be costly, but it would better to pay the overtime than to take a cut in what they were going to pay us."

"That was the reason you missed the forecast?"

"That and the general uptick in chain hotel building. We just didn't see that coming. Nobody in the business thought it would be as big as it was. All of us had more orders than we expected."

"You need to get a better handle on those things."

And with that, Linda turned away from Elizabeth and began looking at her computer screen again. Elizabeth stood at the doorway for a moment and then concluded she had been dismissed.

As Elizabeth left Linda's office, she glanced over at May Chandler, who rolled her eyes in sympathy. Elizabeth knew she should be used to such abrupt treatment by Linda after having worked at Arttekko for thirteen years, but it bothered her every time.